Penguin Crime Fiction
Editor: Julian Symons
The King of the Rainy Country

Nicholas Freeling was born in London in 1927 and spent his
childhood in France. Before taking up writing he worked
for many years in hotels and restaurants, and from their
back doors got to know a good deal of Europe. When
Love in Amsterdam, his first novel, was published in 1962
he stopped cooking other people's dinners and went back
to Holland. His second and third novels, *Because of the
Cats* and *Gun Before Butter* were published in 1963. They
have all been published in Penguins, as well as *Valparaiso,
The Dresden Green, The King of the Rainy Country,
Criminal Conversation, Tsing Boum* and *Strike Out Where
Not Applicable*. His latest books are *The Cook Book* and
A Long Silence.

Double-Barrel, Because of the Cats, Love in Amsterdam
and *The King of the Rainy Country* are all available in
Penguins in the U.S.A.

D1166792

Nicolas Freeling

The King of
the Rainy Country

Penguin Books

Penguin Books Ltd, Harmondsworth,
Middlesex, England
Penguin Books Inc., 7110 Ambassador Road,
Baltimore, Maryland 21207, U.S.A.
Penguin Books Australia Ltd, Ringwood,
Victoria, Australia
Penguin Books Canada Ltd, 41 Steelcase Road West,
Markham, Ontario, Canada
Penguin Books (N.Z.) Ltd, 182–190 Wairau Road,
Auckland 10, New Zealand

First published in the United States by Harper & Row,
Publishers, Inc., New York, 1965
Published by Penguin Books Inc. by arrangement with
Harper & Row, Publishers, Inc.
First published in Great Britain by Victor Gollancz 1966
Published in Penguin Books 1968
Reprinted 1975
Copyright © Nicolas Freeling, 1965

Made and printed in Great Britain by
Hunt Barnard Printing Ltd, Aylesbury
Set in Monotype Times

Van der Valk woke up. His mind was filled with confusion and there was a nasty taste in his mouth, like cheap Spanish brandy. Had he fallen asleep after drinking too much? In an overheated room with no window open? It felt like that. He had had horrible dreams too. And these blankets – he had thrashed about, got all wound up. Obnoxious tangle; he gave a great kick and was astonished; nothing happened. Was he still dreaming? – surely he was not still asleep. It seemed his foot was. Something was wrong: he told his leg to kick but the leg refused. The whole leg seemed to be asleep, from the hip downwards; the brandy tasted vile – where had he drunk that? He must still be dreaming because he remembered things about the dream, and it had something to do with Biarritz. Ha, a holiday in Biarritz – bit dear for the likes of him. Nice idea though – neither he nor Arlette had ever seen the Atlantic coast.

It wasn't a nice idea.

Ham though, he had had bread with raw ham. Not Biarritz but something else beginning with a B. Bayonne, Bayonne; he felt triumphant at remembering. And his dream had had something to do with war. The Spanish border – the river Bidassoa. Soult crossed the Bidassoa, going north. Soult was not much of a general, but then neither was Wellington, who took five years to win a campaign in which every single thing was on his side. Soult was good at moving men but not much good at a fight. He would have to show Soult how to fight.

Stop dreaming and wake up. Well, move an arm. He moved an arm, and the hand touched something very funny. A sort of coarse grass. And a stone, and it felt stony under his head too. He wasn't in bed at all; he had been drunk and fallen asleep on the hill under the hot sun. He could smell the sun; baked grass and thyme. He suddenly recalled, then, a most important thing. He had been shot.

He was a soldier in Soult's army, that was it, and that tripehound Soult had left him here to die on the hillside; he knew it was a hillside, for his head was quite a lot lower than his heels were. Poor heels: poor head. He had been shot, and when one got shot in Soult's army one stayed on the hillside and died, because there weren't any ambulances. Full of self-pity, he cursed. 'Now' – dramatic tears were pouring out of his eyes – 'I'm going to die on some godawful hillside somewhere. I don't even know if it's France or Spain, and my bones will be found by Portuguese plasterers gaining illegal entry to the Republic, and they won't be in the least interested. Going to die, and not even had a shot at the enemy. That romantic imbecile Robert Jordan could say goodbye to his girl and get all nicely propped up with a machine-gun and everything to pop at the Navarrese cavalry, and I have nowt. That's it, that's what happens in books. This isn't a book; this is real.' Weeping with self-pity he reeled off again to sleep. The brandy was fearfully strong; the hillside spun round, and round, and round.

When he woke up again there was a face that had not belonged to the dream. A round, youngish, muscular face, very French, with crewcut hair and rimless glasses. He moved his eyes; a white rolled-up shirtsleeve and a brown arm. Thin delicate fingers were squirting the airbubble out of a hypodermic syringe; the needle turned in the air with a drop on the end of it and pointed itself at him.

'Who are you?'

'Be a good boy and forget about Marshal Soult, will you?'

'Where is he?'

'Dead a hundred and twenty years; we're almost getting to remember him with affection. I'm going to put you to sleep now.' He turned his eye with difficulty past the hand as it dipped out of sight. He was right enough about the hillside. On it stood a faded grey Citroen 'two-horse' and a Peugeot 404 station wagon with a

6

cross painted on it. Yes, Marshal Soult had not known about Peugeot station wagons; what on earth was he doing in this company? The round young face with the glasses came back suddenly.

'I am like the king of a rainy country,' Van der Valk told him. 'Rich, and impotent. Young, and very old.'

'Really? Dear dear, you've been too long in the sun, we get you off Marshal Soult and the first thing you do is quote Baudelaire at us. There there, all gone, all these people. Sleepy-bye.'

*

Next time he remembered waking, though he knew there had been other times, in between, it was better. No bells of Bicêtre, no Soult. Arlette, his wife, instead, her hair wild and tatty-looking, unusually blonde and held back with a white bandeau, so that it almost looked as though they had been on holiday in Biarritz after all. He made a big effort to remember. Arlette . . . Napoleon's marshals.

'My poor boy,' she said to him in French. He thought there might have been a blank again, after that, for when he looked again there was the youngish man again with the crewcut alongside Arlette, grinning down at him. Things began to slip into place; he remembered he was supposed to be a detective and felt better.

'I've seen you before.'

'That's right. Out on the hill. Marshal Soult, remember?' laughing heartily.

'But who the hell are you?'

'I'm Doctor Capdouze. At your service. I will explain. Very briefly, and you won't understand half of it anyway, but that doesn't matter. You got shot. A man heard the shot and was curious about it, because there isn't much round here one shoots with a big rifle. He found you, which was just as well. Being an innocent chap who does his best he gave you some brandy, which bloody near killed you, and ran to get me; I'm the village doctor, ha, of St Jean. We brought you away and you're not going to die this time; you've had several litres of blood belonging to Arabs and black men and lord knows who. You're in Biarritz, in a nice clinic, ha, not the clink, though there are some policemen who want to talk to you. Don't worry, I won't let them in yet. You are perfectly all right. In case you can't recall you are Inspector Van der Valk of the Amsterdam Police and this is your wife Arlette. I have no idea what you were doing on the hill, but I can answer for it that you are now surrounded by modern post-operative care, social security, nuns, me, Professor Gachassin who is your surgeon, and your wife who is a remarkably nice woman even if she does come from Provence. O.K.? Nothing more to worry about; you're going to go on catching up with your sleep.'

Van der Valk slept.

*

Arlette did not talk about the rifle-shot, but he stitched information together. He had been shot somewhere near the right hip, with a highspeed Mauser cartridge – whee, that was a whacking great thing, ten-seventy-five millimetre; he had been awfully lucky. It had hit him at a range of about three hundred metres, sideways and downhill; that had saved his life, because the shooter had not known how tricky it is to sight downhill. The bullet had perforated an intestine, luckily just missed the big artery, touched his spine, bust his pelvis, and popped out somewhere in his buttock, leaving a great deal of havoc. He would stay paralysed quite a while, but they didn't think permanently. Doctor Capdouze was red hot, doctors just didn't come any better; all the local people agreed on that. This Professor Gachassin was a big authority from Toulouse, and he had sworn that within a year Van der Valk would be walking again. There would be a long long time, with lots of books and lots of remedial exercises.

'We'll get him up on skis,' they had said. Arlette had suspected that this was talk to cheer her up, but was beginning to feel hopeful. She thought the idea of skis would amuse him and give him something to fight for.

He didn't much like the idea, though he did not tell her that. He

8

had remembered the whole story, by now. Skis came into it. Too much.

As soon as he felt lucid he had himself asked for the police. They turned out to be an elderly commissaire in a grey suit with a scrap of red cord in the lapel, with short grey hair, who smoked cigarettes in defiance of the nurses. He was about fifty, brown and sun-dried as a Smyrna fig.

'Lira, commissaire. How are you?'

'I'm fine: seems there's a hole in my arse you could drive a truck through. Give me one of those cigarettes.'

'Hell, boy, you're not allowed to smoke.'

'Neither are you, here.'

Mr Lira wasted no time arguing. He put a cigarette in his mouth, lit it, removed it with a scarred brown hand, and put it very neatly and delicately in Van der Valk's mouth where it wiggled as he talked. From time to time the French policeman took it out with equal delicacy and tipped the ash into the fresh air outside the open window, along with his own. Each time he had a trip of a dozen steps, which he made without irritation, as though he were accustomed to taking trouble over tiny pedestrian things. Which, of course, he was.

'I understand that you went after a maniac with a rifle for me, and I'm very grateful, because it might otherwise have been me lying there. Strasbourg, though, can't understand why the two of you came haring down here. What was the point? Just to get over the border?'

'There's a man called Canisius, business man. He was here. He went into Spain to look at houses he owns. He was coming back a little later. The idea was to pop him. Going into the hills was with a suicide idea, I thought. That's why I followed. Was I right?' Lira nodded.

'We knew nothing, of course. Only that there was someone up on that hill with a rifle, who could use it, too. We strung boys out with guns, we got a mental doctor from Hendaye, and a loudhailer. Useless. We went up when we heard the shot. Toe job. No head

9

left at that range. I have to make a report for the parquet. I can't make head or tail of the story I got from Strasbourg; you know the story, it seems. If you can just tell me what you know. Anything that looks good on a report.'

'Nothing I know ever looks good on a report.'

'I can see,' said Mr Lira with no smile at all, hardly, 'that policemen are much the same where you come from as where I come from.'

'I'll tell you,' said Van der Valk. 'It's easy really. And now, there's nothing to hurry for. I can't right now. Have to think a bit first. I'm bloody tired. Can you come tomorrow?'

'Yes.'

'Bring me some cigarettes. I can hide them. People keep bringing me flowers.'

Mr Lira threw two cigarette-ends out of the window and stood looking down at him.

'Boy, did you have a narrow squeak – when you're better we'll drink to that. I'll bring you cigarettes.'

'Bugger off now,' faintly.

A nurse came banging in very suddenly, the way they do, stopped dead and sniffed.

'Smoking by god. Policemen . . . like a pair of silly kids.'

'Sister,' said Mr Lira quietly, 'did you know there's a defective rear light on your little Simca? Get it fixed, there's a good girl.'

*

Van der Valk spent twenty-four hours between waking and sleeping, thinking. This was the end of the story that had started 'Once upon a time, in a rainy country, there was a king . . .' The end had not happened in a rainy country, but on a bone-dry Spanish hillside, three hundred metres from where Van der Valk had left a lot of blood, some splintered bone, a few fragments of gut, and a ten-seventy-five Mauser rifle bullet. Only a few more hundred metres away was the spot where Junot had crossed the Bidassoa, going south, where seven years later Soult had crossed, going north, where a hundred and fifty years later the last of the marshals had

10

waited for a Dutch business man called Canisius to stop his car at the border, lying with a rifle in a patch of scrub.

*

Van der Valk had been in his office in Amsterdam, minding, mostly, his own business, when Mr Canisius was announced on the phone from the concierge's office downstairs.

'Wants to talk to someone in authority, he says.'

'What's he look like?'

'Sort of a rich guy. His coat's got a fur collar!' The policeman at the reception desk had closed his glass partition and could not be heard in the passage. Not that Mr Canisius was trying to listen; he was contemplating his beautifully polished black shoes and looking bored.

'Send him up to me,' said Van der Valk.

It was a cold day in early March. Month of cold light dry days and cold wet blowy days. Month of colds. Van der Valk hadn't a cold, but his pockets were full of Kleenex tissues folded small and put there by his wife, which came flying out like a conjuror's pigeons every time he searched for an elastic band or an odd peppermint.

'Are you the duty inspector?'

'I am. Van der Valk is my name; would you like to sit down?'

Mr Canisius would like to sit down: he had not an athletic aspect and there had been two flights of stairs. Yes, he looked rich. The fur collar on the overcoat was black and sleek, his grey bird's-eye trousers were dim but expensive, his shoes were handmade. Nothing showed of his top half but a Paisley silk muffler, though the careful cut of the overcoat hid, Van der Valk rather thought, a prosperous little tummy. He had a grey trilby hat lined with white silk; it had a blonde leather band stamped with gold paint, looked as though bought ten minutes ago.

The face was not particularly memorable, but it was impressive – big and bald, a Roman nose and very black eyebrows, large flat ears with long drooping lobes, wide pale lips with a droop at the corners, drooping flesh under alert little dark eyes that did not

11

droop. Mr Canisius took his gloves off slowly to put in his hat, and at least threequarters of a carat of diamond winked from a pale bun of a hand with little bunches of black hair on it. The voice was veiled and rich, like a Wiener Mélange coffee with chantilly cream floating on the top.

'I must ask you to listen to a slightly unusual tale.' He was taking his time about lighting a short torpedo cigar, dark tobacco; Brazilian or something, thought Van der Valk. There was a faint flavour, not quite a smell, about Mr Canisius, of vanilla and expensive coffee beans, or was that just the force of suggestion? 'I will develop the background briefly' – putting away a thin gold lighter. From a kind of inverted snobbery Van der Valk put a cheap French cigarette in his mouth and lit it with a match. He had a perfectly good lighter, which had needed a new flint for three days now. Words were coming rapidly from a practised lucid speaker.

'You will have heard of the firm colloquially called the Sop-exique. The founders made a considerable fortune in the last century, in undeveloped countries. It is a trade company with considerable interests in South and North America, and fewer, I am happy to say, in the Africa where it had its beginnings. The founder of this firm was called Marschal, a name unfamiliar to you. The name is still represented by a Monsieur Sylvestre Marschal, who inherited and expanded a very great fortune. There is real estate in Paris and Rome, in New York and Rio – I will quote no figures, but you may take my word for it that this is one of the largest fortunes in private hands anywhere. I say private, for it is distinct from the holdings of the company, in property and invest-ments, which are themselves very considerable.' A short pause to let all this sink in.

'Monsieur Marschal is a man still vigorous and active. He is now over eighty years of age, but he visits the Paris office daily. Some few years ago he settled, for reasons I need not go into, a very large proportion of his wealth upon his only son, a man at present forty-two years old. Jean-Claude Marschal lives in Amsterdam, where the office of the Sopex is administered by me, and is the head of publicity and public relations, for the European offices.'

'That sounds quite impressive,' said Van der Valk; there were bits of this story he felt he had heard before. 'Is it?'

No smile, but a slight slow nod of appreciation.

'I am pleased you asked; the question shows you to have some judgement. No, Inspector, it is not. The Sopex is largely an investment trust, and where trade is still carried on it is principally in raw materials. We make no electrical equipment, no washing powders, no breakfast foods. Our advertising budget is laughable and our public relations virtually non-existent. Everybody has heard of us and nobody knows quite what it is we do, which is just the state of affairs we like. However, I do not wish to give you a notion that Mr Marschal is an incompetent tolerated because of his name. He is an able and intelligent man. His work, which is largely meeting, entertaining and communicating with the men all over the world with whom the company does business, is extremely efficient. He draws an excellent salary. He also commands the very large fortune I have mentioned, income from which flows into balances held in banks throughout Europe, in many different names. An arrangement made at varying times throughout his life by his father, at times of political unrest. '

Quite so.

'And he's in trouble, is he?' It sounded banal. The spoilt child become the spoilt man. What had he done, knocked a pedestrian over while drunk driving?

'We do not know whether he is in any trouble. He has chosen to disappear. If there is trouble, naturally we wish to prevent it. We do not wish his father, an elderly gentleman in frail health, to know of it. We wish to safeguard a number of things. Health, property, good name.'

'He could not interfere much with company affairs, if I have understood.'

'Naturally not, since decisions are taken in concert. However, the fortune, while of course private, is also a company heritage, if I may put it so. We should not like to see it damaged. There are also

13

personal relationships, informal business footings and connexions – I need not elaborate.'

'Has he any reason or motive to act purposely in a prejudicial way?' bluntly: he was making notes now.

'None.'

'You sketch a man of no great parts, restricted to inconsequential activities in a company he owns, in a manner of speaking. He might feel slighted? Some real or imagined grievance, that might urge him to launch an attack of some kind?'

'You have not quite the right picture,' unruffled. 'I understand that such a conclusion might be drawn, but to say that Monsieur Marschal has no great parts is inexact. He has unquestioned ability. A far greater say in affairs, numerous positions of real responsibility, have been open to him at all times and repeatedly offered. He has always rejected them. I do not pretend to understand why. Business matters have no grasp, possibly, upon his mind. He has always been content with the work he chose. I have only one criticism of him, that he preferred to use his charm rather than his mind.'

'What were his interests? What did engage his mind?'

'That is a puzzling question. I have asked it myself. When young, the usual amusements of a sportive nature. I know nothing of such. He was an excellent horseman, skier, pilot of racing cars. He played polo, sailed yachts – all the conventional pursuits. He was very gifted at all of them, I am told. I am also told that he lacked perseverance, and always loosened the rein at the moment he should have tightened it. He did not want to win enough. It is too easy for me, he used to exclaim.'

'He's married?'

'Yes. I will forestall you and state that it is not a stormy marriage and that there have been no upheavals nor scandals.'

'Does he chase women?'

'In a lacklustre way.'

'You mean that he's occasionally seen in restaurants with other people's wives but nobody has ever got in an uproar?'

'Yes.'

14

'It comes down to this: he has vanished, without fuss or furore, quite simply, with no indication where or why.'

'That is exact.'

'And you simply want him found.'

'Equally. It is puzzling, you understand. There may have been a rootlessness, a restlessness, but it has been replaced by many years of calm and stability. He has shown no evidence of emotional disturbance, is not given to extravagance or a parade of wealth, and is in perfect health.'

'There is one thing I do not see, Mr Canisius, and that is why you come to me. You confirm that he has done nothing illegal. There is no suggestion of fraud or false pretence. He is just missing, and since there is a fortune involved, that is disturbing. I can see that, but isn't this a job for a private detective?'

Mr Canisius smiled then, very slightly, for the first time. He got up and settled his coat, though it had remained precisely buttoned throughout the interview. He picked up his hat and examined it for signs of contamination. Finding none he put it on his head. He drew on his glove.

'I do not think I need answer that question, Mr Van der Valk. I think, though, that you may receive an answer to it.' He bowed slightly with perfect politeness, opened the door, and was gone.

*

Van der Valk shrugged. He scratched his jaw, then behind his ear, reading over the notes he had made. There were any number of possibilities. The man could have had a row with his wife without it being public. He could have done something to make him the victim of a blackmail attempt. He could have just felt like getting away from it all for a while and forgotten to tell anyone. Mr Canisius might have told him a lot of eyewash. Good grief, there were a million tensions or disturbances that might exist in the life of a very rich man to explain his bunking. None of them were of much interest to him: his job was the detection and prevention of infringements of the criminal code in the city of Amsterdam.

He shut the notebook and picked up a file he had been

interrupted in reading. He then felt a tickle in the middle of his back; a hair must be lodged there. This was altogether more complicated and interesting; with his free hand he dragged at his tie, undid his collar-button and poked a pencil down the back of his neck. Mr Canisius was interesting, and so no doubt was Mr Jean-Claude Marschal, and it was all very mysterious, but the tickle was altogether more urgent.

The pencil was not long enough. There was a wooden ruler somewhere; he was hunting for it in a drawer when the phone rang.

'Van der Valk.' There it was; he slid it down luxuriantly and slalomed with both shoulders.

'Hoofd Commissaris here,' an elderly fussy tone, familiar to him. He left the ruler sticking where it was; this was the head of the Amsterdam Police, and his Commander in Chief.

'Yes, sir.'

'You're the desk duty officer over there, are you?'

'Yes sir.'

There was a long pause as though he were talking to someone with his hand on the mouthpiece. Old boy's voice sounded a scrap querulous. Had there been a complaint again about the towels in the washroom getting dirty so quickly? This was just the kind of thing that would bring out all his Highness' administrative and detective talents. Van der Valk hated those towels; they were the horrible mechanical type that buzzed and clicked when you pulled at them, and then let you have a grudging ten centimetres. Last week he had given a brisk jerk, and brought the whole damn lot out like a huge hateful roll of lavatory paper.

'You have had a call from a certain Mr Canisius.'

So there the wind lay.

'Yes sir. Missing person.'

'You will act upon this request, Van der Valk. Yourself, personally, immediately. You are detached from your normal duties; your superiors will be notified. You will take steps to find this missing person.'

Well . . . That was categorical enough. Was it really his Highness

16

that had decided he would be a good choice for finding missing millionaires? Or was it conceivably Mr Canisius?

'Ha-hm. You are not permitted to use official transport or official channels. Your expenses will be allowed, within reason. You need no help. You will work quietly, discreetly. Courtesy, Van der Valk, caution, tact – quiet. You understand, hm? Is that clear? Despatch, energy, acuity – but quiet. Hm?'

'Perfectly clear, sir.'

'You may be called on to cross the frontier. That is authorized. No authorization for any appeal to the administration in this or any other country unless circumstances expressly demand it.'

'Yes sir.'

'You can begin at once. The sub-inspector will take over your duty. The Commissaire will be in his office this afternoon.'

'Understood, sir.'

The voice had a rasping, nagging note, worse than lavatory towels.

'Mr Canisius expects you at his office at two this afternoon.'

'Very well, sir.' The phone had clanked crossly. Well ... Thunder on the left was, as far as he could recall, considered a bad omen by the Roman augurs.

Mr Canisius, or the Sopexique, whichever way you cared to read it, possessed one hell of a drag. They didn't need publicity; oh dear no. They picked up the telephone, and asked for the Minister.

Big firms did that, of course; there wasn't anything immoral about it. He recalled a recent case, not unlike this one; a fairly important brick in one of the huge industrial pyramids who vanished on his way back from a conference in Paris. The whole police apparatus of the entire country had been turned out, with remarkable speed, and the man had been found a week later in an obscure waterside village. The very simple explanation was that the poor bugger had gone off the rails with overwork and had been within a sheet of paper's thickness of going mataglap; his psychiatrist had prescribed an immediate complete break and a fishing-rod. So distraught had the wretched fellow been – pity the poor executive – that he had forgotten even to tell his wife. She had rushed about bedevilled with anxiety and the press had got the whole tale.

The press hadn't got this one.

There is also a difference, he thought, between ringing the bell for a rabble of country gendarmerie and going on tiptoe to the Chief of Police with instructions to detach a full inspector of the criminal brigade, quietly, courteously, tactfully. With all his expenses paid, of course! Poor old Highness must have really had his arm twisted.

The inference was, presumably, that the Sopexique had just as much drag or more as a firm that was a household word over the entire world. If whatever was good for General Motors was good for the nation it was also a logical conclusion that whatever was bad for the Sopex was bad, very, for several nations.

Which was not exactly going to make things easy for him . . .

He went on scratching with the ruler while he made notes. He decided that the courtesy campaign had better begin with going home, having the best lunch he could lay his hands on, putting on a clean shirt, asking his wife to pack a weekend case, and immediately having a quick super-de-luxe haircut. He would then put on his new suit, very dark brown, from Olde Englande – he didn't know who he mightn't be meeting.

*

The tourist, getting the quick rundown on Rembrandt, is told that what makes the city of Amsterdam notable is, firstly, twice as many waterways and bridges as Venice and, secondly, the very fine seventeenth-century architecture. It is true that at a time when the glories of Paris and Vienna were still to come, when the political capital of the world was Madrid and the diplomatic and artistic capital was Venice, Amsterdam was the world's commercial and banking capital. The tourist, seeing little evidence of all this, is inclined to be sceptical. For with less intelligence than Venice, less than Innsbruck, less even than St Malo, the city fathers have allowed the automobile full liberty and destroyed practically all the beauty.

There was beauty; there was a great deal. The money-grubbing materialists of Amsterdam were among the world's foremost art patrons; they loved beauty and paid money for it. If artists died broke or in the workhouse, like Hals, or sold pictures to pay the baker, like Vermeer, it was not altogether the fault of the money-grubbers, for these vulgar bankers and burgomasters built themselves superb houses and filled them with beauty.

The houses can still be seen, lying in a tight neat belt around the heart of Amsterdam in four concentric circles. The Singel, the Gentlemen's Waterway, the Emperors' Waterway, the Princes' Waterway. Puffy names that sound ludicrous to our ears: these men were, however, all they claimed.

The friends of the automobile claim that the belt strangles Amsterdam. They would like to see all the waterways filled in and made into ring roads, with Underground Parking Lots. The city fathers squirm and snivel, and do nothing.

The beautiful houses are degraded and squalid, and nothing is left but the façades; the insides have been devoured like cheese by the cheesemites of a dingier and pettier commerce than that of the seventeenth century. In each house there are four or five three-ha'penny pricecutters, and as many worthy people crammed into garrets, politely called flats, above. Sometimes a very-important-business has spread its fat bottom over a whole house, and embellished it with a Reception Hall, and massive-marble-and-mahogany, and curly bronze letters, and safes with Deeds, and an air of weight suitable to Atlas.

There are plenty of bombastic nobodies, Delegations and Missions and Consuls, and there are plenty of slummy shysters. If there are two or three of these lovely houses in private ownership still, it is a little miracle.

As far as Van der Valk was concerned there were none. (Does not the Palace of Justice itself take up several hundred metres of hydra ugliness along the Prinsengracht?) He had been in many of these houses to sort out anything from a fraudulent book-keeper to a phony palmist, but private ownership on the waterways encourages nobody's eyes. The houses will be blind and shuttered, with a door that never opens, for against the basement railings bicycles are piled like bones at Verdun. Typists and clerks clatter on the minuscule cobbled pavement all day long. The business men's famous autos are stacked along the water like the tins of salmon in a grocer's they so resemble. There is dust and straw and dirty newspaper, amid which dogs and humans sniff and pee and rummage about. Vans bump and grind; there is a horrible racket, a bad smell and no room at all. Van der Valk, stepping delicately like a cat, arrived at the offices of the Sopexique, which had, of course, a house to itself.

There was a very small, very highly polished brass plate, and immediately inside the door, allowing room for one thin person to put his mouth somewhere near the concierge's forbidding peep-hole, there was another door, armour-plated and massive, that would yield to nothing but a teeny button that lived under the concierge's bunion. He showed his card, murmured, and waited humbly while checking went on over the telephone.

Mr Canisius lived in an office like that in many very rich businesses. It was clean, tidy and quiet, and had at least the merit of no pretensions at all.

'Sit down . . . I will tell you outright that I do not wish you to question the staff here. I have made very careful inquiries. No eccentricity, no irregularity has been found whatever.'

'I will tell you something, equally outright, with your per-mission,' said Van der Valk, pleasantly and politely. 'I will question whom I please, discreetly, according to my instructions, or I will go quietly and catch the plague and you can find someone else.'

Mr Canisius smiled very faintly.

'I make no restriction outside this building. I will give you the addresses of Mrs Marschal, a doctor, a notary, and the last person known to have spoken to Mr Marschal, a man with whom he was friendly. You must take my word for it that nobody in this office can help you.'

'I'll take your word with pleasure right here and now. What I learn elsewhere may change my mind.'

'In that case I will give you my home address. Telephone if you

20

wish, come to see me if necessary – but do not, please, call or telephone here.'

'Who had most to do with him, here?'

'His personal secretary. Very well, she is a discreet person: I will allow the exception. Outside the office, please.'

He picked up the telephone.

'Twenty-three. Miss Kramer? I wish you to meet someone this evening for a short talk. Five-thirty? Café Polen? – that suit you?' to Van der Valk. Nod. 'Take that as settled, Miss Kramer. I need say no more, I think? Thank you.'

Van der Valk stood up, took the piece of paper handed to him with neat writing upon it, tucked it in his breast pocket, bowed and opened the door.

'Telephone me from time to time, Mr Van der Valk,' came the polite murmur. 'Shall we say at least once a week. I am always at home. Oftener, if you have anything of importance.'

He nodded and closed the door.

The piece of paper had 'From F. R. Canisius' engraved on it. It carried the firm's Amsterdam address, was banknote quality, and had no little pictures or slogans whatever.

Mr Canisius lived in a dinky villa well outside the town, the kind that has glass walls and photo-electric cells to open doors, but all the other addresses, he was pleased to see, were within a couple of hundred metres of where he stood.

At the notary's, he was let in straight away, treated with freezing distaste in the darkest office he had ever seen, as dim and dreary as a pine forest in Lapland on Midwinter Day, and told nothing whatever. The private affairs, financial circumstances, testamentary dispositions and family relationships of Mr Marschal were no concern whatever either of the police, or the Sopex, or all the Canisiuses in creation. He left with a flea in his ear and a suspicion that Canisius had known this all perfectly and staged a tiny trap for him.

The doctor was a lot more difficult of access, but a great deal more forthcoming. Not that it helped.

'I gave him a routine checkover once a year, and apart from

that he consulted me occasionally for something banal like laryngitis. Constitution of an athlete, lived a regular and pretty sober life, no weaknesses whatever. Sorry I can't help you. No handy medical way out, I'm afraid. No epilepsy, syphilis, tuberculosis, nothing. No neurotic fears or fantasies – or if he had he never told me about them. Anything disabling I'd certainly have noticed. You can rule out a fugue, or any sort of syndrome. No physiological disability at all; heart, lungs and liver of a man of twenty. Psychological troubles . . .' Shrug.

'Did he ever consult a doctor of psychiatry or whatever, to your knowledge?'

'No, not to my knowledge. I'd be surprised, frankly. There'd be a certain neuropsychic pattern. He'd had various slight injuries, ski-ing accidents or whatnot, but no disturbance or dilapidation. If he hadn't better health than you and me put together, my dear inspector, I'll eat that telephone directory.'

'When was it you last saw him?' A file was flipped through.

'Last October, a little virus infection; there was quite a bit floating at the time. August, renewal of vaccinations. February, a back-garden strep throat. Three calls in thirteen months.'

'Many thanks.'

'Many regrets.'

Mrs Marschal was only just across the road in the Keizersgracht. He had not been surprised, since there are plenty of expensive flats there, but he found a house; a blind closed wall of aristocratic privacy. He had read of such things but never seen one. He walked up steep stone steps, a bit awestruck in spite of himself, and found a bell with some difficulty, concealed in intricate but pure baroque wrought-ironwork.

Nothing happened, and he got a feeling that he had been observed through a periscope and put down as some yob, selling things and knowing no better than to ring here. He had nearly given up when a soft voice surprised him; his back was to the door.

'Monsieur wishes?'

Astonishment; there stood a majordomo, in full classic costume, striped yellow waistcoat and all. Nestor?!

'I should very much like to see Madame if she is at home. Here is my card.'

'I am sorry to disappoint you, sir, but Madame cannot receive you unless she is expecting you.' Courteous regret, in the correct, pedantic Dutch of someone who has learned the language off gramophone records.

The answer is, of course, to say 'Police' but he had been told . . . Was this chap perhaps Spanish?

'I hope,' he said slowly, stumbling a little in his elementary Spanish, 'that Madame agrees when she looks at the card.' On the back he had written 'Canisius'.

A smile, through the mask of courteous gravity.

'I am Portuguese, Monsieur. I will certainly ask. Excuse my hesitation; the instruction is formal. If Monsieur will give himself the trouble of coming in . . .'

He was in a hall, tall and narrow, with a pinkish marble floor and painted walls, apple green and pale gold. Panels of white stuccowork; bunches of grapes and vineleaves in low relief. At the back of the hall was a door, more of that pure wrought-iron repeating the vine pattern. Through this door vanished Nestor.

For a good moment he stood open-mouthed, for he had never seen anything like this in his life; then he walked gently forwards and tried the door. It did not yield; this was the house of very rich people indeed, and burglars might be tempted: doors had secrets known only to owners, Nestor, and the Holmes Protection Company. The house was absolutely noiseless and noiseless too was Nestor's return.

'Madame will be happy to receive you, sir. Allow me?' The door opened and Nestor paused on the bottom step of a stairway. 'Will Monsieur have patience for just a moment longer?'

Beyond the stairway was a small formal orangery. To his right, facing the foot of the stairs – they were the same pinkish marble, with a fragile balustrade that was either iron or bronze – was a niche or alcove, in which stood a small marble nude. He knew very little of such things: could it be a Rodin? There was a bronze boy at the foot of the stair, that was supposed to be looked at from the orangery. Or one could climb the steps and look from above. He was ten steps high, still open-mouthed, wondering if the bronze could really possibly be Donatello, and jumped when a voice spoke just behind him.

'You are quite right; they are there to be looked at, in just that way.'

He turned, a scrap confused. A woman in a silk housecoat was standing on the steps. Narrow vertical stripes, olive-green and silver-grey.

'Sorry – I was staring admiring.' She had his card in her hand, which she gave back to him, with a careful slow look of appraisal.

'That does not matter in the least. Perhaps we will go in here, shall we?' She opened a door beyond the stairs and waited for him.

'Please sit down, Mr Van der Valk, and be quite comfortable. You have plenty of time? Good. So have I. Would you like some port?'

'Not just by myself.'

She gave him a slight smile. 'Oh no. I like port.' She did not ring, but went to do it herself.

It was a small formal sitting room looking out on the orangery; a sort of morning room. Walnut furniture, grave, simple and pure, that was certainly English and he was fairly sure must be eighteenth-century. His father would have known – the old man had been a cabinet-maker – he wished he were here to see this and tell him. The chairs and sofa were in a rusty rose brocade: there was no carpet, the room didn't need one. The floor was plain polished oak boards.

The label on the bottle said 'Smith Woodhouse'. He couldn't see the year. Did it matter?

'Your good health,' said Mrs Marschal, sitting down.

He took a sip of port and thought, furiously, 'Now why did that halfwit run away from this?'

Perhaps it might be the woman; he studied her. Clear skin: clear classic features, but cold for some tastes. Dark noisette eyes, a lot of dark hair held at present in a velvet bandeau. Figure looked quite full; one couldn't tell in a housecoat. Manner polite, even warm. There was a foot in a leather slipper; a glimpse of neat instep and neat ankle. Lot of blood, lot of race, lot of breeding. Sat very upright – convent trained.

'You liked the statues,' reflectively. 'You like this room?'

'Very much. English? Eighteenth-century?'

'Hepplewhite. That piece there is William and Mary.' She sipped her port. He drank his, feeling slightly tipsy already, and it wasn't only Smith Woodhouse.

'We are going to get along, I do believe,' she said to the floor, 'I really do believe.' He said nothing – what was there to say? 'It would make things a lot easier ... Did you know that the naked girl is by Rodin?'

'I didn't, but I did think it might have been.'

'We are going to get along ... You're plainly enjoying that, have some more. Get it yourself.'

Pouring, he had a crafty peep at the year. Nineteen forty-five!

'Mr Van der Valk, what do you know about your errand in this house?'

'That your husband is missing. That I have been asked to find him. Beyond that, absolutely nothing.'

'Was that really all Mr Canisius had to say?'

'He gave me a brief superficial sketch of a life and a character.'

She pushed her lower lip out a scrap.

'He has not a high opinion of either, and he isn't necessarily right. He is only a business man after all. One day – before I knew him better – he was drinking tea here from Sèvres china. I told him it was Sèvres, since he asked. His immediate reaction was to tell me that three isolated Sèvres dinner-plates had just brought an unheard of sum at Drouot. Soul of an auctioneer. My husband knows about such things and loves them. There's a strong Jewish streak in that family, though they get furious if you suggest any such thing.'

'You want him back?'

'That is a fairly complex question. It might be for everyone's good if he came back. Since he has gone deliberately, I am not sure.'

'You don't think, then, he'll come back on his own, eventually?'

'That is hard to say, even for someone that knows him as well as I do. I don't think he will. I could be wrong.'

'He got sick of being in leading strings?'

'No, Mr Van der Valk, you've only had Canisius to go on. It isn't that simple.'

'Perhaps you could tell me more.'

'I had decided that it would be a waste of time to tell anybody anything. Perhaps I am mistaken.'

He was wide awake now, sharpened by Smith Woodhouse, Rodin, and William-and-Mary. She didn't want him to look for her husband. She hadn't wanted to call the police and it hadn't been her idea. There had, of course, been no suggestion made that she had brought about this disappearance. Or that she had anything to do with it. She plainly didn't like Canisius. That gentleman, very likely, didn't care much for her. He had no particular interest in Jean-Claude Marschal, though. Why had Canisius called the police?

He had a lot of understanding to do. A policeman, by the law of averages, gets his experience from ordinary people with ordinary jobs: they are quite complex enough, but one starts at least with a common background, a common set of impressions. One has had after all a very similar life; everybody in Holland has a very similar life. All this experience counts for nothing when you meet the very rich or the very poor. So poor you live in a bidonville, which does not exist in Holland, it is not allowed. To be as rich as this is not allowed, either. This house was a fortress against hostility and incomprehension: that could explain this woman; she was not necessarily a criminal.

'I want to convey to you, simply, that this is not simple,' she said slowly. 'It is of very little use just asking me if I know where he went.'

'Do you know where he went?' The little half-secret smile again.

'You want to tell me that you'll make up your own mind about how simple or how complicated it is. It is your job, and you don't want a silly woman making things more difficult. Very well. I'll show you around. You can make up your mind. I will make no comments and I will tell you whatever you ask, with nothing hidden, if you want it that way. All about him. Read into everything just what you please – conclude what you wish.'

'Tell me about you.'

He must have looked uneasy, not quite daring to smoke in this room, where it might not be allowed and where there were no ashtrays. She saw this. From the William-and-Mary piece the port had come from she got a silver box with a wooden tray inside it that made a perfectly good ashtray, and a wooden box holding Cuban claros. Her movements were quick and athletic; she didn't ring for any footman. There was also a box of very large kitchen matches. The arrangement would have been Jean-Claude's.

'I live alone in this house. I have two children, both girls, away at school in Belgium. You see that there are no more Marschals.

'I am Belgian. My name was De Meeus, my father was a baron. I used to be a ski champion. Champion means you are among the ten best. I had a bad fall when I was twenty-one, but I can still ski. I met my husband at a time when he was also among the ten best. There was a lot of opposition from my family – all that money, and from pretty dubious sources. The old Marschal, Jean-Claude's grandfather, was a very nasty person, I imagine, hand in glove with everything shady. They certainly saw me as something to increase their respectability. Get on good terms with the monarchist money as well as the republican. They never pretended to become castle-owners or landed squires – too smart. They knew they'd look foolish and Marschals, Mr Van der Valk, never allow themselves to look foolish. Never try to humiliate a Marschal – a lesson I had to learn early. The old man, my beau-papa, is a very tough nut. It is very much his business. Canisius is just an accountant, an organization man. A nobody.

'The business, though, bores my husband stiff. Always did. He didn't feel humiliated at being just a master of ceremonies because he couldn't have cared less. Money to him is a tool like a hammer, to drive in nails with. It doesn't drive him.

'He went to a public school, in England. I've sometimes wondered whether that didn't do him a lot of harm . . . he never learned any philosophy. I don't pretend to understand him, you know. Not completely. But I can tell you that his whole life has been a ferocious pursuit of something that would satisfy. His sensibility is very fine, very fragile. He is possessed by passionate enthusiasms every now and then. They absorb his whole life for three months, and then they are dropped, because he is blunted from over-eating. Crazes for sports, for arts, for exploring or mountains or whatever. Never has it satisfied his thirst. Not just pleasure, you know. He isn't a vulgar voluptuary. I don't know what it is he lacks. How often haven't I sat with him at a show or a spectacle and heard him mutter ragingly, "How can they bear to sit here?" Anything bad or stupid, pretentious or false, was shameful and humiliating to him. And how often haven't I sat with him on a terrace somewhere watching a lot of people enjoying themselves – more mutters – "How do they do it, what is it they see, they feel?" – ready to scream with envy. He just utterly lacked the gift of being happy. He had no simplicity. Nothing was ever perfect.'

'Mr Canisius told me he had sometimes "pursued women in a lack-lustre way".'

'I hadn't credited the grocer with that much observation.'

She thought for a while, as though struggling with herself. 'Come – I will show you something. I want to show you that I haven't anything to conceal and that I am not ashamed of being humiliated. Jean-Claude had no inclination towards crime, but he tried various vices at one time or another.'

She was walking up the stairs; there was no sign of any servant, or were they trained to keep out of the way?

'How many servants have you?'

'Four, inside the house. The majordomo is married to a typist at the Portuguese Embassy. The cook, my maid – they are sisters – and a housemaid.'

'Any living in this house?'

'No. They all live in a house we bought for them and had made into flats. There is a gardener, but he never comes inside. This is my bedroom.' It was quite plain and unremarkable. No fourposter that had belonged to Napoleon, or anything. She led him on without comment.

'This is my bathroom,' colourlessly. Ah – they'd saved it up for in here.

It was twice the size of the bedroom, and must have been one of the biggest rooms in a big house. One long wall was all wardrobe, with sliding doors. These were faced with green marble – he couldn't see how thick the layer was. The floor was a more broken yellowish-creamy marble, with streaks of dark red in it. The room was surprisingly warm: he stooped suddenly and laid his hand on the floor – yes, electric wiring underneath.

The bath was a small sunken swimming-pool. Swimming . . . well, it was five metres by three; it was white marble, this time. There were steps at one side, at each end were fountains – one was made out of a huge boulder. Maybe several boulders; he couldn't see. He didn't know what rock it was, nor where the water came from, dripping down on all sides in musical tinkling trickles. It was rough and creviced and shaggy and seemed very old. It was a moss garden, a fern garden, and lord only knew what those plants down there were, probably South American orchids or something.

The other fountain was dull green bronze, a little slim naked figure, a psyche. Mrs Marschal must have turned a tap somewhere; two plumes of sensitive wavering water fanned out from the psyche's upstretched hands; it was as though she strewed blessings, or light, or warmth – he didn't know.

Down the other side of the room ran a slight airy colonnade. There were more statues but he didn't look at them; he had had all the statues he could take for a while. The ceiling was marble too – a sort of cracked uneven paving – upside down! More moss grew there. Light came like rosy-fingered Aurora from behind the colonnade: he could not help it, the whole thing, he was forced to admit it, had beauty.

'Still I gazed and still the wonder grew,' he muttered crossly.

29

'It kept him happy for a remarkable length of time,' she answered in a dry murmur. 'You don't ask what it cost?' maliciously.

'If it didn't matter to him it doesn't to me.'

'For that you shall have a reward.'

Jean-Claude's bedroom was on the far side. It told nothing at all; like his wife's, it was modern, tidy and without extravagance. There were plenty of things like clothes, hairbrushes, and cufflinks, simple and expensive, and he had left them all behind without a glance. He wanted his evening shirt-studs to be real black pearls and not just jet, but they meant nothing to him; the only things that interested him were the things one couldn't buy, like peace or the green Dresden diamond.

It was the same story everywhere. There was a beautiful library, with a Matisse, some of those very good cigars, a splendid collection of Beethoven records, and some fine morocco bindings, any one of these to an ordinary man like Van der Valk the summit of a life's ambition. It was all rather pathetic.

'Did he spend much time at home?'

'Yes. There might come a time when he was out every evening for a fortnight, and there came other fortnights when he never put a foot outside the door. He liked it here, and he liked me here. Peculiar as it may seem, he was very attached to his wife. She was, I say without any pride, the only woman who had any meaning for him. She failed, somewhere.'

'Was there anything in his behaviour at all that struck you, in the days – weeks, if you like – before he went?'

'No. He just went, silently. No scene, no edginess, no pointer at all. He was as he always is, and one morning he was not there. He took nothing. Which means nothing, since he has virtually unlimited money and can pick up anything he fancies anywhere – down to another bathroom.'

'One stupid, obvious, rude question that I have to ask. Were you ever unfaithful to him?'

'No. I am, oddly, quite Spanish about such things.'

'Thank you very much indeed.'

'If you give your name on the telephone, this house will be open to you at any time.'

'Again thanks. May I ask your name?'

'Anne-Marie.'

*

He walked back towards the centre of the town, uninterested in all the antheaps that were disgorging. Daylight was beginning to fade, and as each traffic light turned green the incredible crowd of bicycles that astonish every stranger to Amsterdam surged forward like the charge of the Light Brigade. He paid no attention.

> *'Anne-Marie, que fais-tu dans le monde?*
> *J'irai dans la ville, où'l y aura des soldats'*

Professional skill at keeping appointments brought him to the door of the Hotel Polen at precisely five-thirty, despite bicycles. Miss Kramer was not hard to recognize, a stocky woman of fifty with a bush of greying fair hair and a tweed suit, standing just inside the doorway clutching a huge secretarial handbag and the sort of secretarial shopping bag containing a folded raincoat, indoor shoes, knitting and the raw materials of the coming evening's supper.

'What would you like?'

'Might I have whisky?' Just what he liked, a robust woman with no nonsense.

'Two whiskies, please. Well, you know what I'm after.'

'I have thought and thought, but I can't recall anything the least unusual. He was as usual, in every sense. He was always quiet and polite, not at all a difficult person to work for once you knew his little ways.'

'Was he talkative at all? I mean that some men in the little intervals of their work chat vaguely about where they've been, who they've seen, how they feel. With you, was he open or closed?'

'Closed on the whole, but he did talk to me – it wasn't just grunts all the while like some. I mean that he mentioned things and people. Not much; just enough to be human.'

'Remember at all what he talked about the last day? A person, a thing, a book, a play?'

'Nothing specific that I can recall. It was one of those very grey lowering afternoons when one almost thinks it will snow again, and I had to turn more lights on, and he said something about how dismal the town looked. I mean it was just a vague remark with no particular bearing.'

'What did you say?'

'Oh, some inconsequential remark.'

'Yes, but what?'

'Well, I come from Brabant, you see, and I said something about there at least one had the carnival at this time of the year to cheer people up and give them some gaiety. I miss that here in Amsterdam.'

'What did he say to that?'

'Oh just vaguely that yes, a carnival would enliven things a bit.'

'And there was no oddity or tension at all? Nothing harassing or especially boring?'

'Not at all, I'm afraid.'

'I'm very grateful.'

'Not much reward for a whisky.'

'Do you know his wife at all?'

'Never even seen her. He never mentioned anything private – don't think he was the type to weep on his secretary's shoulder. I liked him; I miss him a lot.'

'Who is doing his work?'

'I am, most of it. Not the dining and the wining.'

'I won't hold you up. What have you got for supper?'

She laughed.

'Scrambled egg with deep-freeze shrimps – pretty dull, I'm afraid.'

'Good appetite.'

*

He still had to ring the Amstel Hotel. Mr Libuda was back, and could see him straight away if he cared to come. Remembering

32

suddenly that his expenses were being paid, he took a taxi. Mr Libuda was in the bar, and bought the whisky.

'Yes, it was about this time of day – let's see – it was today a week ago. We had dinner here – I had to go to Köln the next day. Came back yesterday – glad to be out of that, I can tell you. Carnival!' Of course. Today was Monday. The last Monday before Lent. Rosenmontag in the Rheinland – high jinks in Köln.

'Did you mention it while you were with him?'

'He reminded me, now that you mention it. I'd forgotten all about it. I was groaning and he said he liked carnivals and I said rather he than me. Good grief, I left Rio to get away from all that Mardi Gras lark.'

There was no more to be heard from Mr Libuda, and it probably didn't mean anything at all. Still, it was a crossbearing of sorts. It was the only damn one he had. He went home, taking the tram this time; the rush hour was finished.

＊

There was ham omelette with spinach for supper, and the television showed snips from the carnival-gallivanting in various corners of Europe, including Köln, Mainz and München. The Germans were all roaring about happily in cowboy suits, and the beer was going down glockglockglock; herr jé, how did the German bladder stand it?

＊

He went to the office next morning with the bored feeling of a lot of tedious routine jobs to be done, and so it proved. The day was spent with airline and shipping bookings, car-hire firms, hotel fiches. A whole damn day, and at the end of it a vague certainty that Jean-Claude Marschal hadn't just gone off to some obscure corner of Holland to do some fishing.

'I hear you've got a nice soft job out of the private bin,' said Chief Inspector Kan cattily, meeting him in the corridor. Van der Valk cursed halfheartedly.

Towards evening time he got an idea. Jean-Claude Marschal had served during the war with a British Army Intelligence unit. Nothing spectacular: rank of major, the usual fistful of decorations, no wounds. Nine tenths of it desk work; still . . . Had he ever done anything special? Was there any corner of Europe where he had been parachuted or infiltrated or rowed ashore in a little rubber dinghy? Anything that might give him a nostalgia for a time that had been less boring? Van der Valk rang up the War Office in London; they were quite polite in a sticky way, and once they overcame a natural inertia they promised to get him off a night letter.

Anne-Marie had promised him photographs, and on his way home he picked them up. None were very recent, but the bony face with the sharp nose was not one that would change a great deal. It was even fairly distinctive; there was something about that nose that reminded him of somebody-but-he-couldn't-say-who – it would occur to him later.

More jollification this evening; climax of carnival, under the cold, dry, bitter, dusty north-east wind. Holland watched the goings-on with a confusion of disapproval, envy, and a slightly concussed horror.

'Turn the rubbish off, it gets on my nerves,' said Arlette: she was dressmaking in an angry way peculiar to herself, with vicious snips and clashes. The tock of her thread breaking sounded like an arrow in a target; her machine had a sudden nervous whirr like partridges in stubble. There was an anguished squawk as she ripped a length of cotton across. He studied the map of Europe. Mr Marschal had a French passport. If he was in Holland he would surely have shown up by now; nobody was sleeping under any bushes in carnival weather. He had left his little Panhard coupé behind. Where was he? Or was he dead?

If one went places, to get away, to flee, to withdraw, to be alone, did one go to a place that held a special kind of memory?

Why had Mr Canisius been so insistent on bringing the police into it? Could there be any reason at all for suspecting a crime?

Anne-Marie . . . complex woman . . . Van der Valk went to bed to mend his head. Vinegar and brown paper . . .

*

Ash Wednesday. Arlette went to church to have her forehead marked and be reminded that she was dust. He went to the office, with a gloomy feeling that a policeman was reminded daily he was dust, but there was the reply waiting for him from London.

Major Marschal had not done anything fancy. He had worked after the landings as a liaison officer between the British and General de Lattre. He had been at Colmar, Stuttgart, Ulm – the French 'Rhine and Danube' army. Later, under the occupation, he had been De Lattre's contact man with the British commander in Köln – ha ha, the one that had decided that Adenauer must be sacked. Köln again; strange, that. A superstitious person sometimes, especially when he had no facts to go on, Van der Valk was fascinated by the way the name kept cropping up. He had once been there himself, to arrest a gentleman working a cheque fraud. Man had made an amusing travelling companion, though that had not stopped him getting eighteen months.

He had made a friend, too, of the German policeman that had tidied it up for him. Heinz Stössel was as German as his name, but you would have to be up early in the morning to get ahead of him. Poor old Heinz; carnival would be a naughty time; all those drunks in cowboy costume who turned out next day to be company directors. How would Heinz look in cowboy costume?

It was ridiculous, of course; there was absolutely no reason to believe that Jean-Claude Marschal was anywhere in the Rheinland. Fellow was in Switzerland long gone, with a damned great bank account under a code number in Zürich. Enjoying that healthy diet of milk chocolate.

Still, he had been told not to make official inquiries, but nothing had been said about the old-boy network. He picked up his telephone.

'Police Praesidium, Köln. Hallo? Any chance of finding Stössel in his office? May not be gone yet? – put me through anyway. Hallo? Heinz? How are all the cowboys?'

A deep dramatic groan vibrated the diaphragm.

'Gets worse every year – dustbin men swore they'd go on strike, three taxi-drivers were attacked, we had one hundred and forty-seven auto thefts and the bill for broken glass is astronomical. The insurance people refuse all carnival claims on principle – they say it comes under civil war. Over now – I love Lent!'

'How's your trade in missing persons?'

There was a sudden silence.

'Why d'you ask? I have a very naughty one but it's not on your teletype yet. You clairvoyant or something?' The voice sharpened suddenly. 'You haven't found a girl, have you?'

'No. I've lost a man.'

'You've come to the wrong address, son. We've lost a girl – and the press got it before we did.'

'Yes, that's the worst sort.'

'There's worse still – we've just found her clothes in some woods. You can see the headline – Naked Beauty Disappears!'

'Any starting point?'

'Precious little – a barman saw her the night of Rose Monday with what is described as a handsome middle-aged man. Now you tell me your troubles. I haven't seen any signal, but to be honest I've been too busy to look.'

'It isn't on the teletype. It's one of those confidential jobs. Man's a millionaire.'

A groan of disgust.

'And I suppose he's handsome and middle-aged, is he?'

'I suppose he could be called that – by a barman. I'm not seriously suggesting it: I've got no pointer at all. But the name of Köln has come up three or four times in an oddly peculiar way. The thing is that just before he ducked my man was talking vaguely about the carnival.'

'So was everybody else.'

'Do you believe in coincidence, dad?'

'You got photos?'

36

'In my pocket.'

'Not much though, is it? Handsome middle-aged man. You might as well say he had a glass of beer and a cowboy costume.'

'I'm going to catch a plane.'

'Are you serious?'

'My expenses are guaranteed.'

There wasn't any need to tell anybody, even Heinz Stössel, who would understand. There were two things driving him. One was simply the wish to get off the ground: he had had a feeling already for twenty-four hours that he was going round and round and staying in the same place. The other was pure wishful thinking. Like a poker player, with a fistful of rubbish, who discards three and keeps two miserable small hearts; by wishing hard enough he feels certain that his three new cards, turning them cautiously, one by one, corner by corner, up towards his twitching nose, will be three more hearts. Occasionally, they are.

He rang the airport; no space on the afternoon plane, but one at midday. He went home to pick up his bag, regretting the impulse a little already: it meant that instead of getting dinner from Arlette he would get a plastic tray with thingummybobs in aspic, and dry salad, and a huge piece of pastry with whipped cream that had gone slightly cardboardy from being kept in the fridge – he knew that airport food!

He didn't believe Mr Marschal was dead: he didn't believe in any crime: he couldn't accept that the man was any sort of criminal. Yet because he heard a nonsensical tale about a naked girl and a handsome middle-aged man he went haring off to Köln. I am like the man in the Bible, he told himself, who strained at a gnat but swallowed a camel. Or was that in the Bible? Not that it mattered.

*

In Köln there was a message from Heinz. He had gone home to get some sleep; he would meet Van der Valk this evening at six on the Rhine Terrace. Here, in the meanwhile, was a transcript of the meagre facts available.

The girl was seventeen, rising eighteen. Her name was Dagmar Schwiewelbein – the kind of name a German sees nothing comic in. She was described as extremely pretty. There were photos available but they were misleading, apparently; the girl had shot up suddenly and changed her hairstyle, plucked her eyebrows, done all sorts of things the parents disapproved of. These parents were very quiet, simple honest folk. Father was clerk in an insurance office, a very nice chap, not conspicuous for brains. There was an elder brother in the army; the girl had lived at home with her parents. They were utterly distraught, of course. They had brought their daughter up simply, innocently; she had always been quiet and good, an honest little German girl wearing an apron with little pockets in the shape of hearts, and her hair in ringlets. Not an outstanding schoolgirl, not bright enough to go on to a higher school. She had taken a job in an expensive flashy shop as countergirl, selling sports clothes. She had never been away from home till last year, when she had gone with two other girls on a wintersport holiday; her hobby was gymnastics and she was mad on ski-ing. She had never had a regular boyfriend, though she had been to the cinema with various young hopefuls. A good, quiet, innocent girl.

The parents had not liked the job: she had got hard and flashy, 'like all the other girls nowadays', and sometimes wilful and cheeky with her mum.

Last month a big event had come to her life. She had been chosen for the Carnival as a Tanzmariechen.

This is a German phenomenon: the Carnival Prince has a troop of attendants, among them a sort of bodyguard that he carts about with him. These are the tanzmariechen, twenty or so of the prettiest and longest-legged girls in the town. They wear a very fetching musical-comedy-military costume: a kind of hussar tunic, tights, high boots, and a Cossack fur hat. It is very becoming on a tall slim girl.

I can't think about her, thought Van der Valk, as Dagmar Schwiewelbein. I can think of her, though, as the tanzmariechen, which is a pretty name for a delightful phenomenon.

They ride in the parade with the Carnival Prince, on Rose

Monday, and they appear of course at the great ball and banquet. This one hadn't; she had just disappeared. She had been seen that night having a drink with the famous 'handsome man' in a café; nobody had thought anything of it. Nobody had ever seen her again. The costume – recognized by the sobbing mother – had been found in a neat pile in some woods ten kilometres or so outside the town, that were being searched as a matter of routine. There was no sign at all of trampling or a struggle or anything else: just a little pile of clothes. A naked tanzmariechen had disappeared into the cold March wind, veering between north-west, when it inclined to be wet, and north-east, when it was just cold.

Van der Valk trudged through Köln and got as far as the Rhine Terrace. Ash Wednesday – a carnival hangover: the streets seemed empty, the people slow and depressed. There were scarcely any people in the big glassed-in air-conditioned terrace. There was a view over a glaucous clouded-over Rhine, the huge heavy current even dirtier and more sullen than usual. The totally deserted outside terrace was decorated with flags of many countries, a few upside-down and almost all frayed by the wind and eaten by the Ruhr air. A vast poster announced that the Köln Football Club was host that Saturday to Borussia Dortmund. Banners advertised beer and fizzy lemonade. Another huge poster shouted the praises of the great ancient Roman Kennedy-visited Capital of the Rheinland. Everywhere one looked one saw the familiar twin towers of the Cathedral and the leggy stilts of the Rhine bridge.

Van der Valk didn't want beer, especially not on a cold and dirty day in March. He cast around the bar looking for something else. Schnapps, horrible sweet vermouth, the German imitation champagne called Sekt . . . He saw a dusty bottle on the shelf, of a shape he recognized. Gentian, by heaven. It suited his mood exactly.

'How d'you serve it?' asked the barman dubiously.

'Put some ice in an ordinary water glass. Now fill it half full.'

'First time I've ever done one.'

Van der Valk sat in solitary state, with the headlines on the Naked Beauty, and waited for Inspector Stössel.

'Ha. Beer?'

'No beer. I've only just got up. Coffee.' Everybody was drinking coffee in Köln today – Ash Wednesday.

'Pot of black coffee for two,' Van der Valk told the waitress, standing bored jingling the change in her apron pocket.

Heinz Stössel was like a large unsmoked ham, pale, solid, salted. Fat but firm and healthy. Without his reading glasses he looked dumb, which had deceived many; when he put them on, which he did to drink coffee with, he looked like a wicked and intelligent Roman senator. He stirred his coffee and looked at the Rhine with distaste.

'She's not in there, anyway. Nor in the woods. How serious are you about this?'

'She was seen with the man.'

'Yes. Right here. Drinking sekt. She was in her costume. The barman looked, because she's pretty, you see. Man is much vaguer – thin, ordinary clothes, described as elegant. When a barman says elegant what do you read into it?'

'Suppose that instead of being abducted and raped and maybe knocked off and shoved in a rabbit-hole somewhere she deliberately vanished.'

'But what supports that? Nothing in her character or behaviour to suggest it. The rabbit-hole's a lot more likely, I'm afraid.'

'Look. I have a man. Exceedingly rich. Eccentric. A nervous type. He has gone, just gone like that. There's a possibility of a rabbit-hole there too, but I can't get along with it. Supposing he were here. I've nothing to prove it but he might have been. The vanishing of my man and the vanishing of your girl might be connected. Too much of a coincidence.'

Stössel sipped his coffee. If he was contemptuous of this his face did not show it.

'Yes, but what have we got to show any connexion? Where are your photos? That barman is the one right there – that's why I brought you to this dump.'

Van der Valk spread photos on the counter. The barman looked.

'Well . . . I suppose it could have been. I didn't really look that close at him. Like him, all right. I couldn't honestly say for sure though.'

'What good is that?' asked Stössel heavily, back at the table.

'None at all. Just a crazy notion. I'm quite prepared to admit it's crazy. There's something offkey all the same about the way this girl vanishes.'

'You mean she's not the type quite. Neither is she the type to go running off with your millionaire.'

'No.'

'Let's see those photos.'

He tossed the packet on the table; one slid, a little; the edge of the one above it cut the hairline off.

'Looks like Jacques Anquetil,' said Heinz stolidly. Van der Valk leaned over, and gave a laugh and a shrug.

'I knew it was like somebody. Couldn't think who.'

'The hair changes the whole shape.'

'And if you're thinking of a millionaire you don't think of a bicycle champion.'

The German got up and walked over towards the counter, still stolid.

'It changes things, though . . . Listen,' to the barman. 'You've heard of Jacques Anquetil?'

'Of course.'

'Think carefully. Take your time. Now tell me whether perhaps the man with the girl looked at all like that?'

There was a silence, a funny silence, Van der Valk thought. There is something ridiculous about three people standing frowning, thinking of a set of features as well known as any in Europe: plastered over every newspaper in Europe, on every television screen every day for three to four weeks, every summer. Five times the winner of the Tour de France – that bony, nervous racer's face above the handlebars is unforgettable.

'Why yes,' said the barman. 'He had that kind of hair, and that sort of face. Sort of long and sharp. Sort of hollow.'

'Now look at the photo again.' A ham-like hand was covering the hair.

'The hair changes it. It's certainly like. I wouldn't like to have to swear to it.'

'No, we're not asking you to. Just like or not like.'

'Like. Very like.'

'Fair enough . . . It's not conclusive, of course.'

'No, but smart. Of you.' They were back at the table.

'I've seen it before,' said Stössel calmly. 'Witnesses can never identify a photograph. But they can see the likeness of both to a third person they know. The thing is to find that third person. Jacques Anquetil . . . ' He gave a short snort of laughter.

'Why not, after all ? Must be a millionaire himself.'

'And we can hardly suspect him of the job, huh ?' said Heinz.

'Come on,' he added, drinking up some cold coffee. 'Back to the shop.'

*

'Assuming you're right . . . ' sitting down in an office a lot bigger, a chair more leather-padded, with a lot more ingenious machinery on the desk, than in Van der Valk's office in Amsterdam, but with the same smell. 'Why, would you say ?'

'Does it matter ?'

'It worries me. It seems so out of character.'

Perhaps, thought Van der Valk. You haven't seen that house; you haven't talked with Anne-Marie.

'Let's see if we can work out how.'

'True . . . Planes are out. Taxis are out. Car-hire is out. Train . . . maybe.'

'Car buy, maybe.'

'We'll try,' with a face. 'What might he have had – traveller's cheques, dollars, any idea ?'

'He's not that dim. German cheque on a German bank, likeliest, according to the hint I got.'

'In a German name ?'

'How many autos, though, are paid for cash down and driven away ?'

'We'll make a composite photo and show it around. Come to

42

that, if all this is sound, he might have bought all sorts of things. A house, even. Anything expensive, not in itself unusual, but perhaps seeming unorthodox . . . My god, I'd hate to hear what the Polizei President would say to this notion – I'm suppressing you in my report in any case; you've no official standing.'

*

Van der Valk, with no standing even to read electricity meters in the city of Köln, could not take part in the hawking of a prettily faked photo around the expensive shops where a man looking like Jacques Anquetil might have bought a car, or a house, or a caravan, or . . . damn it, what had he thought of? Where had he gone? Where could he be hidden? It was a difficult thing, to think oneself into the shoes of a very rich man who wanted to cover his tracks.

He went to see the parents of the tanzmariechen. The mother was not much use – poor woman, she was a blur, like a water-colour left out in the rain, and whatever she could manage to tell about the girl was as bad. The father was more help. He was, thought Van der Valk, a man of surprising innocence; he did not even think of asking who this man was that spoke quite fluent German (but talked about das Zeit). A kind man, a man of goodness, simplicity, a man thinking evil of nobody: the girl, thought Van der Valk, had these characteristics too. Might that have struck Jean-Claude Marschal?

*

As they expected, a quite astonishing number of eccentric people had bought eccentric things and behaved in eccentric ways; it had, after all, been carnival time. Every policeman, in every shop, was regaled with tales that went, 'That's nothing, though. Why, I could tell you. There was a man that bought twelve nightdresses all different colours . . . ' It was exactly like the old 'Believe it or not . . . ' column that had made Mr Ripley a household word when they were boys. But nobody recognized the photo, except the man in the garage, who thought it might have been a man he had sold

43

a car just before carnival started, on the Friday: Carrera 1900: German racing silver: a Mr Alfred Kellermann. The man in the garage cared nothing for bikes though, and had never heard of Jacques Anquetil. If it had looked like Stirling Moss, now . . . It was all very vague.

Mr Kellermann had spoken good German, but not like a Rhinelander; more like a South German or an Austrian. The cheque was on a big bank: no information was forthcoming about the account without a court order.

Middle-aged handsome men in red, black, blue and white Porsche autos were reported all over Germany.

'I can't believe in it,' said Heinz Stössel. 'Where could they sleep? They must spend the night somewhere. You don't sleep in a Porsche auto.' He had the stubborn obstinacy, the refusal to be discouraged, that Van der Valk lacked.

'They're over the border long gone. Holed up somewhere in a wintersport village. He was a good skier. She worked in a sports shop and liked it too.'

'It's on the list,' said Heinz briefly. His theory was that you can find anything and anyone with a routine, if that routine is only well enough co-ordinated. Police departments are increasingly fragmented and where they fail is in faulty liaison. A man looked for by, for instance, the fraud squad for a very smooth savings' bank trick may be completely unknown to a murder squad, who would not know him even if they had him in the office as a witness. Heinz Stössel had fired arrows at every department in the organization. Faced with a man who, technically, had committed no crime at all (they had absolutely no pretext for looking up, for instance, the bank account) he had calmly assumed that the man was guilty of every crime in the penal code. He had made a list of everything he could imagine Mr Marschal doing, had virtually every policeman in Germany hunting for it, and had every report made put on his telex. Every hour, he went with his red pencil, line by line, through the reams of tape. He was looking, he said, for a co-ordinate.

'I think there might be something here. It's inconclusive, though.

44

A large quantity of ski equipment and clothes, including some for a woman, was bought in München. The man does not follow our description particularly, but was tall, thin and assured. Knew all about what he wanted. The only thing that really struck them was that at the end he signed a very large cheque without even checking the number of items on the bill. When questioned they said that another thing that struck them was being told to deliver everything to the luggage office at the station. Cheque on a local bank. München looked for any more cheques in the same name. They found one at a travel agency – two first-class tickets to Innsbruck.'

'What's the name on the cheque?'

'Funny name. Nay.'

'Nay?' said Van der Valk. 'Nay?'

'That's what it says on the tape. Nay.'

'Ring them up, Heinz. I am a fool, ring them up, tell them to check the spelling.'

Slightly astonished at this vehemence, Stössel picked his phone up. 'München . . . one six seven, miss, please . . . hallo? . . . hallo? Schneegans? Stössel here in Köln. This cheque in the ski-shop. Did the operator get the name right? Nay, yes. Check it will you? . . . yes? . . . OK, thanks.' He put the phone down. 'Yes, but how did you know? Easy slip to make, can't blame them really. An e instead of an a. Ney. I don't see it.'

'Ney,' said Van der Valk, grinning, 'is the name – it's absurdly childish – one of Napoleon's marshals. Born German – in the Saar. Kellermann is one too. I've kept thinking and thinking what it was that was memorable about it.'

'You mean this is him?'

'Can't be anyone else.'

'Gone to Innsbruck. Looks like a risk but it was safe really. München to Innsbruck! Well . . . what can have happened to the auto?'

'That damn routine of yours,' said Van der Valk, still grinning.

'I had every auto checked,' indignantly. 'Bought, hired, borrowed or stolen.'

'You don't know an auto's stolen, though, till someone reports it stolen.'

'Yes, but . . .'

'What better way would there be of getting rid of an auto you think might be recognized? Leave it on the street unlocked in a town that size – it'll be gone without trace in three hours. You simply never report its loss.'

'What – a brand new Porsche?'

'We just haven't been keeping pace with this kind of mind. That brand new Porsche means about as much to a fellow like this as a Dinky toy.'

'I see. No wonder we missed him . . . Anyway, we've got the two linked. We know now that he went off with the girl. Find him, and we find the girl. Or the other way round. I need to get the President, now, to ring up Innsbruck.'

'No need. I'm going to go there myself.'

'You've no authority, though.'

'I don't need it. All I have to do is walk up to him and say the party's over. The whole drama will collapse and the girl will just come home. What can it be, after all? Just a whim of a rich man. A romantic escapade. She'll have come to no harm. But he'll be watching the German papers, Heinz, amusing himself, I've no doubt. Don't let the press get it.'

*

It was like passing from one world into another, he thought, in the plane. He hadn't been able to tell Heinz, but everything there had been out of key, the scenery and lighting false and melodramatic, the shadows exaggerated and distorted, the feeling of the whole atmosphere wrong. If a girl disappears, there is a possible crime; if the girl is not raped, or murdered, or sold into slavery, or something, well, there remains an abduction. The distraught parents, the screaming press, the hundreds of policemen and firemen and soldiers in high boots peering under bramble bushes – everything gets out of hand. Jean-Claude Marschal had committed no crime. He had to keep reminding himself of that, but he was sure it was true; Jean-Claude had quite likely never even realized that the German police would take it all so seriously. To him getting a girl to run away with you was a new sensation, a new thing, a new experience. That was how it looked; he didn't know, himself. Jean-Claude had run away; he had known or guessed that he would be searched for. Really searched for? By the police? He had hidden himself cunningly; it had taken Heinz Stössel's fantastic routine, with threads from the whole of the Federal Republic twisted into a lasso by a teletype, to find him. It hadn't caught him.

Van der Valk was distracted momentarily. First by the stewardess, who had so much hair that he wondered for several moments how on earth she managed to keep her cap on, and then by the beer he asked for. It was perfectly good beer, but by the peculiar snobbish alchemy of airlines it was Danish. Because, he thought indignantly, we are flying at three or four thousand feet over the territory of the Federal Republic, German beer becomes immediately too proletarian for the likes of us – and I shell out four and sixpence for a gold-label Carlsberg as meek as Minnie Mouse. Indignation at this meekness had to simmer down before he could concentrate on Marschal.

Marschal must surely realize that the police hunt for persons reported missing. He might have reckoned on Anne-Marie making no fuss; she hadn't wanted any police – she'd made that clear enough. He must, too, have thought that Canisius would be unperturbed – and there he had made an error. He had known that his absence made no difference to the business, and he had known that as the heir to the Marschal fortune he was a person of importance in everyone's eyes. Conclusion was, surely, that to fall into the error of supposing that Canisius would take no steps towards having him found he must have imagined that Canisius would be glad to have him gone, out of the way, forgotten even.

Not only had Canisius taken steps – he had taken very drastic steps. An inspector of the criminal brigade had been detached, with wide powers and all expenses guaranteed. As though there had been a crime. Yet there had been no crime. Yes, persuading a girl under age to run away from her home was a legal offence, but Marschal had not thought of that. Otherwise he must have known that the police would look for this girl, as well as for him. Had he thought that the girl would confuse everything, providing him with a kind of camouflage?

The beer tasted good. Van der Valk reflected that Canisius was paying for it, just as he was for the plane ticket, and cheered up.

Could Canisius have known or guessed something about this girl? That hardly seemed possible. Could he have known or guessed that Marschal might do something of the sort? Something wild, something unstable? Had they known of some secret, some inner flaw in the man? Was that why Canisius had insisted on an inspector of the criminal brigade? And if that was the case, why hadn't he been told?

Was Marschal unbalanced? Had he perhaps done something criminal in the past? Could this German girl be in any danger?

No no. He shook it off; that was worse than unsupported theorizing, that was senseless vaporizing. The Head Commissaris of Police in Amsterdam might be a nervous civil servant, but he would have satisfied himself that there was no crime. If there had been anything criminal, he would have followed the routine pattern, Interpol and all the rest, and he would not have departed from it for twenty millionaires. No, his Highness had behaved in a way that was plausible enough. A millionaire with amnesia, who must not be chased or harried, who must be looked for very quietly and discreetly by a responsible experienced officer – with all his expenses guaranteed – that magic phrase had been enough to quieten his Highness's conscience, no doubt!

It was a grave mistake to get himself hot and bothered about motives, thought Van der Valk. He was an inspector of the criminal brigade: very well, that simply meant that he was a policeman like any other, acting under orders, orders to look for a man, find him, and simply report his whereabouts to Canisius. These orders were not affected by anything he might not know: even if the man were a criminal, it was irrelevant. A little thread had brought him to Köln, where a friendly gesture had put a whole country's police apparatus in movement for him – Van der Valk knew very well that Heinz Stössel had not, until the discovery of the second bank account with a Napoleonic name, been very convinced that Mr Marschal was responsible for the disappearance of little Dagmar Schwiewelbein. Out of goodwill he had summoned a monstrous expenditure of energy (with sufficient excuse to explain it to his superiors) and had got a positive result, a clue to Marschal's whereabouts, inside forty-eight hours.

The next little thread, in Austria, might take a bit longer, but Van der Valk knew well enough that he would find his man. The frontiers were being watched; Stössel had sent a signal about the missing girl to the police of Innsbruck. He would find him easily enough, and then he would make a phone call, and that would be the end of it. Canisius would come, or send a confidential minion, for a little chat with Jean-Claude. The German girl would be sent home, and any possible criminal charge concerning abduction would be politely forgotten. An incident . . . Jean-Claude Marschal was not a criminal. There had been no crime.

And Anne-Marie? Would she thank him for all that? She had not been any too enthusiastic at a policeman, however responsible, however experienced, however tactful and discreet, running after her husband. She had yielded eventually, become more open, but she had not lost all suspicion. She had agreed that Marschal should be followed up, but she had made a clear hint that Jean-Claude was not an ordinary person, and a clear appeal to him to make an effort to understand, not to accept everything he was told. Just because he had had some vague clue about those statues, some vague notion about the famous Hepplewhite furniture? Of course not, but she had thought him a little more able than most to realize that this was a peculiar bird. 'I really do believe . . . ' she had said . . . What was it exactly that she really did believe?

Was it possible that . . . ? Why, exactly, had Canisius sent an inspector of the criminal brigade? Could there be something more to all this than met the eye?

No, no, and no. He knew nothing, he was simply going to obey orders, follow instructions, Jean-Claude Marschal has not committed any crime, not even that of abduction; Marschal was not a criminal.

Jean-Claude Marschal has committed no crime . . . It was a bit like the famous phrase in *Liberty Bar*. William Brown was murdered . . .

The plane bumped very slightly on concrete, taxied, turned, roared its engines, and relapsed into silence; everybody hustled for the door. The air was stinging cold and there were mountains all around. This was Innsbruck.

*

First of all, Innsbruck was a great deal fuller than he had thought. He got a hotel room, but not without a struggle. Next week, apparently, there would be the final big international competition of the ski season, and the whole of the 'white circus' would be on parade. The place would swarm with lookers-on and hangers-on, there would be journalists and photographers. And there were, still, any amount of holidaymakers. March or no March, there were forty centimetres of snow right here, and a hundred and twenty on the slopes . . .

There he was, too, deep in the forty centimetres, with town shoes, and a silly light overcoat that had looked perfectly all right in Köln, but here was absurd. Very well, the Sopex was paying the expenses. He was supposed to find Mr Marschal, but nobody had warned him that he might have to paddle in the snow. He went into the first shop he came to in the Maximilianstrasse, and bought himself a mighty pair of boots, and a lovely loden 'canadienne' jacket. They tried to sell him the whole damn shop, scenting a novice.

'I could do with a St Bernard dog.' That shut them up.

Once equipped he had to make his routine call on the police. They weren't a bit interested.

'Fine place you've picked. We've got all the hotel registrations, naturally, but the valley's full of chalets and houses that would take a year to check. You don't see that, but all these mountain districts are the same. People own a house, good. We know their

50

name. They let it for a month, the tenants sublet, the subletter camps a dozen pals in the kitchen – do you think we know their names? We don't even get the tourist tax half the time.'

The commissaire's name was Bratfisch. He was rough and tough; rough blond hair, a rough tweed jacket, a pair of shoulders made to burst in doors, and boots like Van der Valk's, made to kick people out of them. Van der Valk leant back in his chair, with his hands in his pockets, and chewed on a matchstick. It was just the fellow's manner, he thought. Plus a message. You damned policemen from the towns in your clean white shirts may think yourselves clever, but don't think that we bow down before you. We are mountaineers.

'It isn't really my fault that they came here, though,' softly.

'Ach, of course not. Just that this can't be done one-two-three. Firstly, your birds could be in the Vorarlberg by now, or in the Engadine. Second, they can get very worked up in Köln about a girl that's disappeared but here, one has to realize, these things are a daily occurrence. You know how many girls reported missing I've had here since the season started? I'll tell you – eighteen. The air goes to their heads. They get seduced by beach boys and fall off the tree like cherries. Six weeks later they turn up at their consulates without a sou asking for a ticket home.'

Van der Valk did not mention Jean-Claude Marschal. He knew what answer he would get. That a missing millionaire might be a horrible great headache to some finance company but that all the millions wouldn't put more than twenty-four hours in the day.

Bratfisch obviously felt he had been a little too uncooperative.

'I'll help you all I can, naturally. Next week it'll be different. This last few days is the worst. Last classic of the season. Blame it on the mountain air. The old women are the worst. They dress up as though they were twenty, leave money and jewels all over their hotel rooms, walk off a terrace leaving mink jackets on the backs of chairs – you know how many people come each year new to the winter sports? Twenty per cent over the year before. And you know what it is here, since the Olympics? Forty per cent. Every man I have is up to the ears and short of sleep. Next Monday the circus will be gone. Try me then, if you haven't found them. Servus.'

'Servus,' said Van der Valk. He wasn't particularly bothered.

*

They weren't being disagreeable; it was all perfectly true.

Look at those old women in the tea-room there, gorging on whipped cream. And as for handsome middle-aged men – even if they weren't handsome they looked it in brilliant sweaters and tight ski-trousers: you couldn't see their hair under knitted ski-caps, and you couldn't tell whether they were thirty or fifty; and if they hadn't had girls when they came they had now. German girls, English, Danish, Finnish girls: the Innsbruck Anschluss was as classic as the Kandahar Run.

The wonderful new snowboots were hurting his unaccustomed feet; he hobbled rather over the creaky snow. 'Snow White and the Seven Dwarfs' he muttered, catching sight of his reflection in a round knitted cap with a bobble on the top. But at least he no longer stuck out in this crowd like Miss Bikini-Bust.

The reception desk was full of people writing picture post-cards. He asked for a telephone line to Amsterdam, was told there would be an hour's delay, and went into the bar, where he drank gentian and took his boots off surreptitiously in the dim light under the table.

'Mr Canisius? Van der Valk here. Speaking from the Hotel Kandahar at Innsbruck. He's around here somewhere. He was in Germany. He went off with a girl. Yes, just picked up a young girl and seemingly talked her into leaving home without a word of warning. That got signalled, of course, by the German Police. The two are here now. They'll find it very difficult to leave now, because all the borders are on the lookout. I've no doubt I'll find them, but it's still very crowded with holidaymakers here, and it may take some days. Does this news surprise you?'

'Not at all,' came Canisius' voice, dry, level, practised at speaking over long-distance telephones. The line was astonishingly good: mountains or not, he could have been in the next room. 'It is exactly the kind of unbalanced act I had feared. A possible scandal looming. Now you know why I was emphatic about discretion. Do the local police know all this?'

'They know about the girl. That is the pretext for my inquiries. Nobody knows about him yet, though the German police know something, naturally, since I had to tell them. They haven't released anything to the press, though.'

'Good, good. Excellent. I have no doubt that you can find a pretext for keeping Mr Marschal from any further escapades until I can be notified. I will know then what steps to take. I am very pleased that you have got on his traces so quickly; congratulations. Remember, Mr Van de Valk – discretion. He may do something unexpected if he finds himself cornered.'

'You think that he is unbalanced, do you?'

'Don't concern yourself about that, my dear inspector,' the voice was silky. 'Remember that we are all acting for the protection of himself as well as of very considerable interests. Ring me again the moment you have any news. Goodbye now.'

He went and had dinner. He was extremely sleepy from the mountain air, and his leg muscles were aching: he got some stuff from the porter to grease the stiff newness out of the famous snowboots, and put his legs in hot and cold water. But he was a little overtired and overtense.

He had left his gloves somewhere, and would have to buy some more, and snowglasses. He was beginning to understand Mr Bratfisch, especially after reading the local paper.

He could speak and understand German well enough, but this mountain dialect was a bit beyond him; they had all sorts of words for things that foxed him. He was a bit of a fish out of water here: he had never been on skis in his life, and didn't intend to start, thanks, and get shipped home with plaster on his leg. He would have to do a lot of walking, he could see that. In the snow; on the slopes – those poor leg muscles were going to suffer. Too bad about them.

He didn't understand a thing about Jean-Claude Marschal. To talk about being unbalanced . . . Running away suddenly with the tanzmariechen – he was sure there was nothing premeditated about it – was that really unbalanced? Mr Canisius was very quck to say it was. Anne-Marie had remarked that it didn't do to take the word of a Canisius as an infallible guide to understanding Marschal. What sort of a fellow was he? Romantic, impetuous, contemptuous of consequence. There was something paradoxically schoolboyish about a millionaire who has private bank accounts in half the major towns in Europe, keeping them under the names of Napoleonic Marshals. He was giving a romantic dash and sheen to that prosaic money. What was the point? Yes, he thought, he would have to go to the library and get a list of all those Napoleonic characters. Likely as not there was an account here in Innsbruck: he recalled vaguely that there were several Alsatian ones – Strasbourg was a great breeding-ground of marshals – with Germanic names.

He thought about the tanzmariechen. A hussar, a cavalier, almost a Rosenkavalier? Full of innocence, of courage, of trust. What pull could that exercise on Marschal? Did it really mean anything deep to him?

He had had Anne-Marie's word that Jean-Claude had never found any woman but herself that really meant anything to him. He hadn't thought she was lying, either.

If Marschal was behaving in a peculiar way, so was Canisius. Van der Valk had come round again to the old puzzle: what was Canisius so anxious about? Surely an escapade more or less trivial of the son-of-the-family could not seriously worry the Sopex? How did it warrant sticking a criminal-brigade inspector on his tracks? It was as though they were sure he had committed or would commit crimes, as though they knew something he did not know? Or – maybe, maybe – as though Jean-Claude Marschal knew something about them, and they knew it.

He didn't know it. He had again that uneasy feeling that there were too many things he hadn't been told.

What could Jean-Claude have on the Sopex? Or perhaps on Canisius? Some disgraceful fiddle? Some mean murderous strangling of something or someone that had got in their way? A huge tax evasion? Could he have heard or accidentally discovered some fact about that huge enterprise, that gigantic fortune, that had shocked that rather juvenile, immature, romantic spirit?

He didn't know; right this minute he didn't very much care. He turned on his stomach with a deep groan, pushed the pillow around a bit with his face, and fell instantly, heavily, asleep.

*

He was still sound asleep when a tremendous bang at his door announced eight-thirty, chambermaid, and coffee. He sat up yawning and hungry.

'*Herein.*' She was already gone when he noticed that there were two cups. Well, he could eat breakfast for two. With all the anschluss going on, probably Innsbruck chambermaids automatically brought breakfast for two! He was scrubbing his teeth when there was another bang. There you are, silly bitch had brought the wrong breakfast. He struggled with the toothpaste and turned around to find Anne-Marie – calmly sitting pouring out coffee!

'Good morning. I hope you don't mind having a guest to breakfast. Black or milk?'

It took him some time to collect scattered wits.

'You a detective or something?'

'Canisius told me. I acted upon a sudden impulse. I discovered I could get a night connexion, through Paris. My plane landed two hours ago.'

It was all too much to grasp, when he hadn't even had coffee. He felt extraordinarily bleary, decidedly hemmed in. She had, he supposed, a perfect right to appear here, but wasn't it a bit drastic to appear like this with the coffee? Still, one had to admit it wasn't a disagreeable sight. She looked very young: in black trousers and sweater – she was even wearing ski-boots – he saw the girl of fifteen years back, who had married Jean-Claude Marschal. He drank his coffee and felt less woolly.

'Canisius,' she said calmly, eating brioche with apricot jam, 'who thoroughly enjoys telling people things they might find

55

disagreeable, said he had a girl with him. What is it? Some rag-doll of the ski-slopes?'

'I don't know. She comes from Köln. He met her there. She is eighteen years old, a shop assistant, very pretty, good at things like dancing and skating, and her name is Dagmar.'

'You see? – a rag doll,' through another bite of brioche. 'Jean-Claude must be out of his mind. It bothered me. There must be something wrong with him – that's why I came. You don't mind?'

'Madame, he's your husband. I've only been told to find him.'

'It isn't a crime, to run off with little girls in Köln.'

'No. Unless he'd used violence of some sort. Which is extremely unlikely. An imprudence perhaps – if he really didn't want to be found.'

'Wasn't it Talleyrand who said that an imprudence was worse than a crime?'

'I think he was talking about something that was both. I'm wondering whether your husband has ever committed any crime?'

'Why should you think that?'

'Perhaps because I'm a policeman. I have to shave.'

'Go ahead and shave. Don't mind me.'

It was disconcerting. He felt oafish and provincial: this was really an infernal nuisance. Having this woman hanging about would not make things any easier. What was she driving at? Why had she come to drink coffee in his room before he was even shaved?

'Is it impertinent to ask what you propose to do?'

He felt his jaw and put away the razor.

'Have a shower,' he said, picking up his clothes. It must be because they are so rich. I don't belong in this league, in fact I feel a bloody fool. I should be back in Amsterdam, sitting writing reports in the office. I don't belong in Innsbruck; I can't get accustomed to waking up and finding a millionaire's wife by my bed pouring out coffee.

Still, the hint had been broad. She would have gone away, he hoped, rubbing his hair dry and feeling rather clearer.

She had gone away, but she had come back again. On his bed

lay a very gay, extremely luscious, appallingly expensive sweater – the kind of thing the expensive sports shops display casually in their windows, knotted round a pair of batons. He stared at this. She was standing by the window smoking a cigarette.

'What's this?'

'A sweater. That v-necked thing you have is no good here. You need trousers too – I'll get you some. The boots will do.' He stared at the sweater, which was exactly the right colour and extremely tempting.

'I have to tell you two things, Mrs Marschal. First, I am a policeman and can't accept any sort of a gift for obvious reasons. You know, what the French delicately call a pot of wine. Second I don't take things, even in private life, from women. Come to that, I usually drink my coffee in the morning with my wife.'

'Very stupid you sound,' she said calmly. 'If this girl is as stupid as that Jean-Claude will simply put her on the train home. You'll never be able to ski if you stay as stiff and Dutch as that.'

'I don't want to ski. I don't intend to ski.'

'You're on the slope,' impatiently. 'Ski, or stay sitting on your dead arse.' He opened his mouth, and shut it again. Life was too rapid this morning; he was getting old.

'Put it on. You'll look good in it. And don't talk that childish nonsense about "gifts" since I know perfectly well that Canisius is paying your expenses. You came here, didn't you? You took a train or a taxi or some damn thing. Put it on.'

'Are you jealous of him? Or hoping to see him and make him jealous about you?' She just looked at him then, saying nothing.

Well, this was life with the rich; ski, or sit on your dead arse. He picked up the sweater and started putting it on. While he had it over his head he was knocked over backwards by a pair of strong arms and held by something hard and muscular that smelt good: the trouble was that this was not particularly disagreeable. He felt something the way Jonah did, when he saw the whale's mouth open. He got the sweater over his head and took the biggest gulp of fresh air he could get; the arms let him go suddenly. She leaned back on his bed and put her hands behind her head. In an absent-minded sort of way she started doing leglifts with her boots on, to strengthen her stomach muscles.

'I am a capricious, vexatious, nasty person,' she said quietly. 'I have been badly hurt. I hope I see this dancing girl, this beauty, this Pisslinger. I hope I see her in the middle of the Olympic Piste. I'll do some slinging. I'll knock her off her goddam skis.'

He brushed his hair and grinned.

'Very nice sweater, this. I'm going to enjoy it. You're a downhill girl, aren't you?'

'Yes. When I schuss, I schuss. I don't want just to make pretty patterns.'

'He could be anywhere in Austria, you know.'

'There's a competition starting today. The girls are going to run down the Olympic Piste. Draw a big crowd.'

'I see. You sound quite enthusiastic. And you think it'll draw him?'

'He likes to watch the competition girls. Look over this year's crop. Of course, if you want to go running round Austria, that's your look-out. Be a great waste of time. Loosen up, enjoy yourself; don't be so Dutch. This is all unimportant. Can't you see that?'

'Sure. Everything is unimportant.'

'You're taking everything too seriously,' impatiently. 'It's all plain as daylight now. Jean-Claude went off in the mood for some amusement for a change. He picks up this ridiculous doll somewhere and goes off to do a bit of ski-ing. Can't you see that just knowing that is enough? There's no call any longer for all this pompous tracking performance. Forget about that fool Canisius. He called you because he's an old maid. You're here now – very well, profit from the occasion. Amuse yourself.'

'With you,' grinning.

'Ach, pay no heed. That was just a little spat of rage on my part. Jealousy, if you like. I'm a downhill type and I work up voltage.'

'You were one of the competition girls, weren't you?'

'Yes. When it comes to a competition, I can go faster than this Pisslinger, and Jean-Claude knows that perfectly well. What's her real name, anyway?'

'Dagmar Schwiewelbein.'

'There you are. Call that a name?' She laughed.

'The Germans see nothing comic in it.'

'I do, though. For a skier!'

'So you're thinking of just walking up and tapping him on the shoulder.'

'Tell me then, what would you have done, if I wasn't here to find him for you?'

'Oh, quite a boring long routine,' he said calmly, watching her. 'One sets a machine going in a given area. Go through hotels, restaurants, chalet hire services, garages, shops, the lot, if necessary.' No need to tell her how little enthusiasm the Austrian police had for all that – between Salzburg and Feldkirch!

'You see?' she said, shrugging. 'It's perfectly imbecile. Just as though he were a gangster or something. Forget you're a policeman. I'll teach you to ski.'

'Very well,' he said calmly.

Who did she think she was kidding?

*

The downhill girl! Very well, he would stick to her; there was truth enough in her tale to make it the right move. Undoubtedly she did want to find Jean-Claude, and undoubtedly it was easier to find that gentleman with her than without her. In a crowd he might not recognize the man at all. She would, though! Naturally, he knew he could find Mr Marschal even if he had to look all the way from Salzburg to Feldkirch: people have to eat and sleep somewhere, and Marschal had expensive tastes. . . .

But it would work this way. He was pretty sure she was right, and that the two were in Innsbruck or near by, and that they had left a track that she knew how to follow. He had not said anything about the bank accounts, but he had gone with her to the bank; she had come in a hurry, and needed to pick up a little money. He found it wonderful that these people took money so for granted; to them it was as natural as water to a town-dweller – you turned the tap and there it came. He watched her making jokes with the teller behind the counter, walking over towards him stuffing Austrian banknotes casually into the sleeve pocket of her anorak.

'You got an account, in Innsbruck?'

'No – Wien.' He didn't take it any further. She got some news there, he thought.

And now they were watching the competition, or rather the crowd. There was no sign of anyone that looked either like Jean Claude or the tanzmariechen.

He had got quite interested in the ski-ing. It was the first time he had seen a competition, and he liked the way the girls hurtled round the curve, biting their skis in to grip the snow, leaning over against the centrifugal force, tucking their batons under their arms and hunching down into the 'egg' for the long run in, rocking slightly to get the last scrap of speed from the slope. It was very fast, very graceful, very exciting.

Anne-Marie had taken a dislike to the girl that had made the fastest time.

'Stump-legged, stump-witted, about as much sex appeal as a glass of stale beer. Always the same.'

'Uh?' There were perhaps ten thousand people, perhaps more, but another couple of thousand made no odds in the huge white valley. A football stadium would have been easier, but there one would have no liberty to walk about. They had started at the top of the hill and worked down: the crowd was strung along the four kilometres of the Olympic Piste and with a little patience one could look at everybody. Around the finishing line at the bottom were no more than two thousand people, perhaps; he had his binoculars on them.

'Always the same,' she was going on. 'The really good skiers, the amusing ones, with a nice style and a bit of flair, get a bad starting number or have a sturz, and something wins with a style like a jeep, all tit and elbows.' Yes, he thought, vaguely, the one he had liked best was the girl who had come slashing down giving herself shouts of encouragement, gone too far out on a curve, done a skater's step on an icy patch and with a huge dismayed howl cabrioled into the crowd like a rabbit. A flurry of anxious hands

60

had helped her up, and she had sat shaking with laughter.

There were still riders coming down, but a ski competition is won and lost by the first dozen, and the fanatics, the ones who were interested only by the performance and not by the spectacle and the atmosphere, what the Germans call the Stimmung, were already trickling down the slope at the bottom back to their autos. He was looking at one pair in particular, perhaps four hundred metres away and fifty, forty below, a rifle-shot, say. That, now, could perfectly well be Marschal and the tanzmariechen; the girl, in a big white fur hat, was in the right clothes for the part; the man was loading skis on to the rack of a red station wagon. The trouble was that a thousand pairs looked exactly the same. He could not see the nose at all, let alone the face; he held the binoculars steady, waiting for the man to turn, when the glasses were snatched out of his hand: Anne-Marie had suddenly noticed what he was doing. The red auto backed with a swirl and shot down the valley road, hidden at once by an awkward clump of pines. He took the glasses back leisurely. It had been a Fiat twenty-three hundred.

'Mark,' he said, contentedly. He had them! They were really here! He felt exactly as though he had drunk a tumbler full of champagne, straight off. His feet were no longer cold and his eyes no longer vague. He glanced at her; she had put on an indifferent face.

'So.'

'I couldn't really see whether it was Jean-Claude or not,' she said. 'He was already stooping to get in – whoever it was.' It was as obvious a lie as ever he had heard.

'The Austrian police can pick that auto up in half an hour.' He had no intention of telling the Austrian police, but he wanted to see how she would react.

'Don't be such a damned idiot,' furiously. 'If you call the police the whole damn thing comes out in the open, just for that silly girl. You can't do that. Anyway you don't need to. They'll be here tomorrow, for the slalom. You can watch out for them – it'll be easy.'

'It'll be even more easy to get them roped in straight away. They could just as easily have seen us – you, I mean.' He knew something would have to give, now.

'You fool, you fool – can't you see that's exactly what Canisius wants?' He was walking rapidly down the slope; she was having to hurry to keep up with him. 'Stop.' He stopped. The auto she had hired was parked in the crowd, perhaps fifty paces from where Jean-Claude had left the red Fiat. 'Please,' she said. 'Please come back in the car with me. I want to explain something to you. Will you just not do anything precipitate till you've heard what I have to say?'

'Very well.' She unlocked the auto; there was the usual stuffy, tinny smell. It was an ordinary hire-service Rekord. There hadn't, officially, been a car left to hire in the whole of Innsbruck: she had got one though. She got things done the way Jean-Claude got them done.

It had been sunny all morning, but it had clouded over now and was going to snow again. Yesterday's fresh snow was lying thick on the whole valley, but the road had been kept free and one could drive fairly fast. She was driving a little too fast, but well. 'Not much of a car is it, by your standards?' She shrugged. 'They're all useless things. I've had them all: I know. I've had Ferraris and Maseratis, I've had a Hispano nineteen-thirty, with a solid stork and an ivory steering-wheel. You get there just as well on a scooter.'

A downhill girl! Or no – he was changing his mind about her: it was more Jean-Claude who was the downhill type. Calmly picking up a girl like that and not bothering his head for a second whether her family would be worried, whether the police would be notified, anything: someone else would have stopped to think. Would he himself not be searched for? And the girl – people were not going to just sit gazing at the fact that an eighteen-year-old girl vanishes. Yet he had not bothered, just come carting off here to Innsbruck and amused himself ski-ing, without a care in the world? That made no sense. There was something that drove him: he wanted to get somewhere fast. Anne-Marie knew about that.

The competition skiers call the downhill run 'the hole'. You jump into it, and once you go there is nothing to stop you but the crash into the loose snow at the edge of the piste, where you can as easily break your leg or even your neck as find yourself panting, shaken, covered in snow, either laughing like that girl today, or crying, like three others that had gone off at exactly the same spot. You know nothing and you think of nothing. You simply get there, on nothing but your muscles and your instincts, at anything up to a hundred kilometres an hour. The top-class men average over ninety along the whole course; the girls hardly less. Competition ski-ing itself is a nonsense, because anybody at all can win, since conditions change in a minute, and the biggest championship can be won by one hundredth of a second. But the fact of going as fast as you can, stopping for nothing, on a course every metre of which can put you in hospital for a year, is enough, for in no other sport are you so close to the magic heart of life. He had seen that, this morning.

No, Anne-Marie was really more of a slalom girl. There are two ways you can run a slalom. You can wildcat it, hoping you hit nothing, or you can run it cunning, taking good care you hit nothing. For those frail stalks with the little fluttering pennants turn the darting iridescent dragonfly back into the shabby laborious caterpillar. They are made, even, of a special flexible plastic, for at the speed of a slalom nowadays a wooden or bamboo stick would be too dangerous.

To him, Anne-Marie was on a slalom course whose flags he could not see. All the movements were like the ski-jargon, meaningless. What was the point of the jet turn and the light christiania, the wax and the fix, the skate and the schuss, when a thick fog of not understanding lay over the whole maze? When he could see no flag?

She stopped outside the Kaisershof, and jumped out without looking at him.

'Come on up to my room. I want to talk to you in quiet, and the place is full of gibbering journalists.'

She had to pause a second for her key. Two of the journalists were waiting for telephone lines.

'I tell you a lightweight has a natural advantage on that kind of gymkhana course,' one was saying.

'What about the long schuss at the end, then?' countered the other. 'Her ten kilos extra picked her up damn near a second on that stretch alone: I clocked her there.' Just so, friends.

Anne-Marie kicked her boots off, flung her anorak at a baroque gilded chair, and picked up the telephone.

'Send up a bottle of whisky and two glasses.' She looked at him. 'Sit down,' abrupt. She walked about, and looked out of the window, where the snow was beginning to fall again. He lit a cigarette peacefully. She was going to slalom, and he was going to guess at the flagstaffs!

'I'm going to ask you to stop. To leave Jean-Claude alone altogether. To go home and forget him. I have a right to ask that. I'm his wife, after all. The rest is pure formalism. Don't bother about Canisius: I'll deal with that.'

'It's not quite that easy. Canisius didn't hire me like a private eye.'

'But you can't arrest him or anything. He's committed no crime.'

'As to that, I haven't been told,' drily. 'I'm a police officer, acting under instructions. Those instructions were simply to find him and establish if possible what he is proposing to do.'

'And why do you think you were given those instructions?'

'I don't need to think about it. My superiors were satisfied that they were justified. We already have evidence that they were justified. Taking a girl away from her home sounds harmless enough. She's under age, though, and she comes under the care-and-protection statutes. There exist in all European countries criminal charges that apply. Never heard of *détournement de jeunesse* – corruption of youth?'

She poured out a big glass of whisky, and drank it straight off, as though to fortify herself in a struggle against obstinate imbeciles.

'Look – when I saw you in Amsterdam I could see you were not a foolish man. You don't believe all this claptrap. You know perfectly that it's a pretext.'

'Certainly. From the first moment I was handed this tale I began asking myself why a man missing from home – an occasion for a police operation that is the simplest routine – was made a reason for sending an inspector of the criminal brigade, which is what I am, personally to try and find him. Without any of the usual steps being taken. No notice to Interpol, no notice to any of the administrative branches whose job it is to check things like hotels. Very unusual. In fact I've never heard of such a thing being done in all my experience.'

'And why, do you think, was it done?' Her voice was silky; her eyes gleamed, probably with whisky. She poured another one into her glass and, as an afterthought, filled the second glass too. She came over and handed it to him; he took it and drank some. Very good whisky.

'I should say,' steadily, 'that a very large quantity indeed of money had something to do with the case. Mr Canisius and his friends are perhaps nervous that your husband may do things that look irresponsible, in the eyes of the world. They might be alarmed at the thought of his being able to run all round the world playing duck-and-drake with what everybody agreed is a colossal fortune.'

'Have you sympathy with that point of view?'

'I don't have sympathies; I'm getting paid.'

She shook her head over him, sadly.

'Use your intelligence. Try to understand.' He drank some more whisky: he was enjoying it very much.

'People who have a great deal of money – a very great deal – are not easy to understand. They do things that people like me find confusing. I am trying to see why a man like Mr Marschal suddenly leaves his home without telling anyone. Why he goes to Köln at carnival time and runs off with a pretty girl in a gay uniform. Why he then sails off to the winter sports and has no cares, apparently, but to look over this year's crop of ski-girls.'

'You are paid to have no sympathies,' she said. 'Here, have some more whisky. Very well. I have, as you remark, a great deal of money. I will pay you to try and be less stupid. You want me to tell you why?'

She had already finished her second glass of whisky. She picked up the bottle, brought it over with her and bent over him to fill his glass up. Van der Valk understood at that moment that an extremely good-looking woman in ski-clothes, drinking whisky in a hotel bedroom with mountains outside the window, is a very tempting object, as tempting, perhaps, as a girl of eighteen at carnival time, dressed in the costume of a tanzmariechen.

'Suppose I was to explain all this to you in bed?' she said gently in his ear. She smelt of healthy woman, and faintly of sweat and perfume. There was the smell of expensive wool from her sweater, of ski-wax, of leather, of whisky. It is the world's most seductive smell.

'Canisius, and the clan, are very clever, you know. Take my clothes off.'

'I can remember the same woman saying to me in Amsterdam "I am quite Spanish about such things." Well, it just so happens – so am I.'

'You think that Canisius has something on Jean-Claude – or on me? Don't you?' She was behind him now, with her arms round his neck. 'You want me to tell you about it. I will show you how Spanish I am – if you like.'

He stood up, took the bottle from the table where she had put it, filled his glass, took a long drink, took a big breath of the scented air.

'Yes,' he said. 'I would like to know several things. I think that Mr Marschal could tell me most of them. I would like to meet him. I want to meet him more than ever. If he's planning to go and see the girls slalom tomorrow, I'll be watching out for him. If he's not there, I'll turn the whole of Austria upside-down and keep shaking till he pops out. The German police, he may not have realized, are watching all the borders. They want this girl back. So do I. Going to bed with you would be very nice, and there's only one thing I want more. To talk to your husband. That, for me, is the important thing. I'm a policeman. What Canisius thinks or does is of less interest to me than what Jean-Claude Marschal thinks – and does.'

66

'Very well,' she said after a moment. 'Very well. You may be right. We'll see – tomorrow.'

'I'll see you tomorrow morning,' easily. 'Thanks for the whisky.'

*

The waiter sat him at a table where two journalists were still drinking coffee, brushing crumbs negligently and explaining that there was rather a squash and tables for one were not easy to come by. Anne-Marie would have got one all right . . . He didn't mind; he would pick their brains and enjoy it. So would they; everybody likes explaining things to the starry-eyed beginner. No lack of openings either; the shoptalk was continuing undiminished.

'Of course she's unbeatable downhill – just that which makes her hopeless between the sticks. Not just too heavy – too crude – she slams the door.'

'Please explain to me how this thing works,' said Van der Valk through a mouthful of bread. 'Just weaving between sticks – it's always seemed dull to me.'

'No no no, just the contrary,' with enthusiasm. One pushed all the coffee-cups away and started to lay a course out with lumps of sugar. 'It just looks like a slope, huh, with snow on it. But apart from all the bumps and hollows, there are lateral slopes from side to side as well, see. Laying the thing out they're dead cunning. The runner shoots out of one gate here, see, and finds himself going sharp downhill and tilted far over to the right. So just to be nasty they set the next gate facing acute left pointing back uphill – so . . . no natural line to follow . . . you've got to pull up against the plunge of your own speed and weight, turn into a fresh line right across the tilt of the terrain, and find the exact angle to thread the next gate – remember five centimetres the wrong way and your ski hooks in the pole – without losing the rhythm. It's tough as hell.'

'And they change the rhythm' – the other was anxious to impart knowledge too. 'They give you a dogleg stretch like he says, gates fairly far apart, and just as you're getting the hang of it they squeeze you into a very tight serpentine bit where the gates are only three or four metres apart instead of ten or twelve, and the runner that can tango like a dream gets buggered doing the twist.'

'Chicken or veal cutlet?' – the waiter, clanking coffee-cups on the tray.

'Veal.' He knew those hotel chickens, trotting tinnily off their assembly line. . . .

'Come on Harry – don't forget the crumpet.'

'Do it no harm to wait a little,' said Harry.

'Anschluss,' explained the other. 'Norwegian anschluss. We teach them to slalom and they teach us to ski-jump, ha.'

'Giant slalom – intervals of thirty metres,' added Harry in a lecherous way. 'Bye now.'

Yes, Anne-Marie's slalom course was quite as wickedly laid out. Why the sudden change of front? Why had she suddenly come haring over to Innsbruck? Why had she suddenly started heading him off and wishing him to lose interest, after she had accepted the notion of his looking for her husband, back in Amsterdam?

Yes, Canisius had told her. Fair enough – normal that Canisius should ring her up, reassuringly. We've got news of him; don't worry, whatever is biting him we'll get it straightened out. But it hadn't been like that. Canisius, making malicious hints about Jean-Claude being in Innsbruck with a pretty young German girl, had said something that had bitten her deep, and he wasn't at all sure that it was just jealousy.

It must have been a shock to her. He thought of her words 'I am the only woman who has any real meaning for him' – and that little spat of rage she had shown over the coffee-cups had not been mere pretence. But was it only jealousy? He wasn't so sure. She had made too abrupt a volte-face – was trying now too crudely to head him off and send him to play with the Norwegian girls. 'I couldn't really see if it was him or not.' What was bad about his meeting Jean-Claude, talking to him, sorting out his tanzmariechen and sending her home to Mum? Surely Anne-Marie could have no objection to that!

Could her behaviour have anything to do with Canisius? Something he had said – or hinted – or implied – or spoken about in a gloating kind of way?

Van der Valk didn't know. He went to ring his wife up, before going to bed.

*

There was a terrific queue for the *téléphériques*. A great many people were going up to look at the slalom course, which had been laid out in two halves down and along the slopes near the downhill track, and the Olympic Piste itself was open again to the public this morning, after being closed for a week for the competition. Several people with their skis on their shoulders were going to go up and see what they could do on the downhill run, excited and emboldened by the exploits of the girls yesterday. A good few of these were nowhere near skilful enough, nor experienced enough, to run a very fast and difficult course, and quite a few might well pay for biting off more than they could chew – with a broken leg or a dislocated shoulder! The Austrians were prepared for that, Van der Valk noticed cynically. They had the helicopter parked at the bottom of the piste; if anybody had a real crash, they used it to whisk the patient back to hospital, and of course, in case one of the competition girls had a bad 'sturz' in the slalom – that happened too!

Round the slalom course and thickest at the bottom, naturally, there was a thick crowd and a lot of excitement. Journalists gabbled, the public gabbled, the loudspeaker blatted. Radio relays were being set up and tested, the television cameras were hamming more than their fair share of space, officials were running about being important with little pieces of paper. The electronic scoreboard was racing lunatically through figures that didn't belong to anybody at all, and the usual regiment of busy little dwarfs was trotting around like ants, pegging in ropes to keep the public back, dumping stretchers at strategic intervals, and staircasing laboriously up and down the twisting track between the gates, patting and fussing at the snow.

Outside the wooden huts with the banners the helicopter pilot was having a flirtation with the dextrose-tablets girl and enjoying a free cup of Ovaltine. And the reporters were dashing to and fro buttoning people, microphones brandished in their hands and hanging on their ties, cables up their sleeve and trailing behind them – they were extraordinarily good at not tripping, flicking the loose festoon of cable out from their feet as a woman flicks a long evening skirt.

There was a lot of tension. Last big competition of the season and this run would decide the combination prize. The Austrian girls had fought for a tiny edge yesterday in the downhill run. Would the French girls steal it back with their better slalom technique? Everybody knew, and was busy explaining why to his neighbour. Van der Valk didn't know, and didn't care. He had found a red Fiat station wagon parked, and was using his spare pair of eyes as well.

Anne-Marie, with her skis on her shoulder, was talking to one of the reporters, whom she knew, it seemed – she knew everybody! She walked back towards him.

'Ten centimetres fell during the night, but married well to the old stuff. Good powder, very fast piste. Icy patches – they think it'll favour the French girls. I feel like having a go – I'm going up to the top.'

'I'm staying here for the moment.'

'Please yourself,' she said.

He turned his glasses on the group climbing into the *téléphérique;* there was a fur hat that had caught his eye. Just such a Cossack hat wore the tanzmariechen. It might be, and it might not be: he couldn't see properly. There was a man with her; might not be – and might be: it was as simple as that. He tucked the binoculars into the top of his zip and took large kangaroo hops down the hill, sliding and plunging. At the bottom it was well trodden; he ran fast.

The crowd had thinned when he got there, and he did not have to wait. The man and the woman were long gone, and Anne-Marie was gone – on the 'bucket' just in front of him. How slow it went – wobbling, vibrating, humming. The sun came out suddenly, amazingly warm in the gripping, biting air.

'That'll put oil on the piste,' said a man next door to him. They

70

had an excellent view of the slalom course, where the first try-out runner was slithering down in a chain of controlled skids.

He leapt off with no skis to wait for or encumber him and ran towards the top of the piste. Yes – there was Anne-Marie, kneeling, doing something with the binding on her ski; he could see her flipping the catch as though she were not quite satisfied with it. Half a dozen people were waiting their turn to schuss, at the top. Van der Valk stumbled through the fresh snow: a runner pushed himself off with an over-ambitious leap, and flew very fast about thirty metres before his arms started to windmill and he hit a tiny hump, lost both legs, and disappeared splendidly into a bank of loose soft stuff left there to make happy landings for the unwary. A knot of boys and girls standing at the top split themselves laughing. He reached Anne-Marie; she had her skis on and as he came panting up she did an about-turn conversion.

'So you did come. Watch me schuss.' They both saw the fur hat together. He gripped her sleeve; two more skiers launched themselves gingerly on the piste, leaning carefully forward, keeping their skis flat: she shrieked.

'Jean-Claude. Jean-Claude.'

He saw the man at the same second; he had been masked by a fat fellow who had let his skis down, done a neat oblique glide, and dug his edges in a couple of metres further. Jacques Anquetil's nose!

Marschal looked only for a second. He saw his wife, and his eye rested for perhaps seven-hundredths of a second (timed by the electronic scoreboard) on Van der Valk. He moved with no hesitation. He put a hand on the fur hat's back, and launched her on the slope. Letting his skis down the way the fat man had done he started a skid, gathered his batons hanging by the wristloops, and went. With professional ease and speed; it was him all right.

Anne-Marie, her batons planted, was tucking her hair under her cap, panting.

'Go on, damn you, go. Catch them up, do anything, stand on your head, but hold on to him. I have to talk to him, I must. Now go, what are you waiting for?'

Marschal had caught the girl up before the turn, swung well out to give her room, and passed her. She was going very carefully; it was too fast and steep for her but she was ski-ing steadily. Anne-Marie went, with a long tearing sigh of the skis, very fast, holding to the line, leaning right over to keep her balance on the turn.

And he could not ski! It had been the same ever since he came here . . . He ran back madly towards the lift, stumbled, skated, and sprawled full length. He ran on muttering furiously, covered in snow, his shoulder hurting.

One of the mountain 'dwarfs' was on the ski-lift; an old man with the thick mountain dialect he could not follow: a puckered, withered, tough little man in a hooded coat too long for him. 'Have a sturz?' he chuckled. Van der Valk dusted the snow off himself and cursed silently. His shoulder hurt. A cheer came up in the thin mountain air from the slalom course.

'We'll flip those French girls,' said the old man.

'Time, fifty-nine eighty-three,' blatted the loudspeaker, but the name was drowned by the echo.

'Who for, who for?' squeaked the old man. 'That's fast, that's very fast.' Van der Valk stared numbly.

They had almost reached the bottom when a second bigger cheer went up.

'Fifty-nine eighty-one, new best time,' bawled the speaker.

'Is it one of ours?' yapped the dwarf, tumbling excitedly off the landing platform.

'Sure it's one of ours,' muttered Van der Valk, limping, his shoulder hurting. 'What d'you think it is, a Martian?'

He loped along the beaten path wretchedly, his heart pounding with the altitude. No fur hat, no nose to be seen at the bottom of the piste, no black trousers and sweater, either. Where had the three of them got to? Three hundred metres further the heli-copter's motor coughed and roared. As he looked it tilted clumsily, lifted off, and turned, gaining height: clouds of powder snow flew about wildly in the wind of the rotor. It roared directly over his head; someone had had a sturz.

He saw Anne-Marie, then, sliding down the last easy slope of the piste. He ran stumbling over to her.

'Where are they?' stupidly. 'How is it I'm ahead of you?'

'I had a sturz,' ruefully. 'A royal one. I looked at the girl instead of the track. Served me right. I flew out at a curve. Lost both skis and all my breath. You had one too by the look of you. Hurt your shoulder?'

He wasn't looking. A new commotion was growing there, on the slope below the crowd watching the finish of the slalom. A knot of people were gesticulating and shouting; a policeman in mountain boots was running heavily, roaring crimson at another, below.

'Someone's pinched the bloody helicopter.'

Anne-Marie laughed, a clear soft laugh with a silver edge of malice in it. Van der Valk would have laughed too, at any other moment; it was the sort of joke he appreciated. It was just this mountain air, and the shortage of breath – he rubbed his shoulder resignedly. Tintin was here . . . It took that; the combination of skill and cheek that comes from having a lot of money. Jean-Claude had taken the girl with him: the tanzmariechen was gone.

Up above, the sixteen runners of the top group had finished the first leg of the slalom.

*

He went back alone to Innsbruck, rubbed liniment on his shoulder, changed, and had time to think what a fool he had made of himself. Floundering in snow . . .

Anne-Marie had shrieked. It had not been a cry of recognition; nor astonishment; nor anger. It had been a cry of warning. There was only one thing that she had not known, and that was Marschal's determination to keep the girl with him. Jean-Claude had seen that Van der Valk had no skis, but that his wife had. The girl had had perhaps thirty seconds start – not enough for a skier as strong and experienced as Anne-Marie. By himself, Jean-Claude could have taken his red Fiat. He had chosen to wait for the girl. In those few seconds – perhaps a minute – he had taken the extraordinarily reckless decision to pinch a helicopter belonging to the Austrian government.

It was not, of course, such a risk as it looked. Nobody pays attention to a helicopter any more; he could put it down anywhere and get a half-hour start. The Austrian police, who were not getting themselves very wound up about a missing millionaire in Amsterdam, nor a missing shopgirl in Köln, would not even be bothered about their helicopter, once they had it back. They would put it down to the exuberance of some student.

He found a bar that was pleasantly dark and stuffy after the blinding white of the snowfields and ordered cognac gloomily. He had made a mess of this. There were a lot of things that were clearer than they had been, at least. That much was gained . . .

Jean-Claude Marschal was bored. He had a boring wearisome life, and found it tedious past belief. That was plain to grasp: the man simply found everything too easy. He had vast amounts of money, and was good at everything. He could win things without trying, help himself to everything he fancied without effort. If he dropped a sixpence, he found half-a-crown lying on the path. There was not much that gave him pleasure, not even vice, not even crime. To run off just because he was sick of everything was quite plausible.

There was more to it. He had been afraid. Canisius had put the police on his track. He had not known that, but he had guessed it. The second he had seen Van der Valk he had known and recognized the menace. Canisius had something on him. A crime – well, perhaps. One did not know. Perhaps an escapade of years before. Suppose – as a hypothesis – he had once had a hit-and-run accident, or something of the sort.

But why, suddenly, should Canisius have become such a menace as to force him to try and escape? If the man had a hold on him, why was it urgent at this precise moment?

Anne-Marie knew a good deal about this. She had not, at first, taken it very seriously, but when Canisius had rung her up and told her . . . He might have been a scrap premature with malicious triumph. When Van der Valk had phoned to tell him about the German police he had been a thought too quick to imagine he had his young friend Jean-Claude Marschal over a barrel.

Now, thought Van der Valk, I am in a cleft stick, for Anne-Marie, who is badly frightened now that she has seen the light, has made a very crude panicky approach: she offered me money, lots of money, she offered to sleep with me – just to forget about Jean-Claude.

And Canisius, for reasons I do not know, will press me all the harder to chase Jean-Claude, harry him, worry him into something still more imprudent, still more criminal. It certainly looked as though Canisius had known what he was doing when he manoeuvred the police into taking an interest . . .

The sensible thing to do is to go back to Amsterdam and make a very carefully worded report, stating just why I think we're being carted and why, at the very moment when I could undoubtedly take Mr Marschal by the collar, I prefer to do no such thing; I don't know enough.

There are several powerful arguments against this. First, it might look a little too much as though I had been sleeping with Anne-Marie – or worse. I have already committed the imprudence of taking a sweater she bought me!

Second, bigger reason was the tanzmariechen. Not only had she been charmed away from her home into what must seem to her a very romantic and glamorous adventure, but Marschal was, for some reason known only to him and perhaps obscure even at that, not letting go. He was cornered now, and frightened. Might he do something even more reckless than pinching a helicopter?

Van der Valk could understand the attraction a girl like that might have to a man sick to death of expensive and sophisticated women: he could understand the excitement of hiding her, smuggling her out of the country, being chased by the German police, taking her off to the winter sports. To someone who found it as difficult to get excited by anything as Marschal, to someone with Marschal's reckless, incurably romantic nature, that was understandable.

But did he love her? How seriously did he take her? Was he aware that she was caught up in a tangle she could not possibly imagine? She certainly loved him furiously, uncaring: for him she would sacrifice anything. But he – he was sacrificing an innocent girl on the altar of his own boredom.

That was the flashpoint – whatever Van der Valk did, he had to get little Dagmar Schwiewelbein back to her distracted parents in Köln. Heinz Stössel was right, Marschal was of no importance: the central figure in this tale was not Jean-Claude the millionaire, nor Anne-Marie de Meeus, ex ski-champion, nor Canisius, regional manager to one of the world's biggest financial trusts – but an eighteen-year-old shopgirl who had put on a Cossack hat and high boots to show off her pretty legs and face at the carnival. Van der Valk drank off his cognac and asked the waitress for a couple of coffeebeans to chew.

*

Mr Bratfisch was sitting at his desk telephoning.

'Quite right . . . no damage? . . . well then, there's no more to worry about, is there? . . . yes of course, but that can wait till this evening . . . Right you are.' He put the phone down, picked up a forgotten cigarette smouldering in his ashtray, and grinned at Van der Valk.

'Well – found your millionaire yet?'

'Found your helicopter yet?' Eyebrows went up.

'So the wind lies there, does it?' He got up and went to stare out of the window. 'Clouding up, and we're going to get a *föhn*. Make the snow sticky. Now if that had happened yesterday we'd have won that slalom.'

'I was out there, but I had other things on my mind.'

'That French sister act again. So it was you. He ran away when he saw you?'

'He doesn't know me. He may have guessed what I am. His wife came here, supposedly to help find him. I was with her. She shouted when she saw him, in a stupid way. We were at the top of the piste. He was on skis and I wasn't. I can't ski anyway; I had to go down on the bucket. He took a remarkably drastic way of getting out.'

'That's of little enough consequence. We weren't worried. You can't hide a thing like a heli. We've just found it. Took us two hours searching, for all that; it was quite cleverly hidden, at the top of a valley in a stand of pines. Might have taken us longer, but we took another heli to search for the first one – since last year, we have two.' He threw away the cigarette, picked up a half eaten piece of bread and cheese, and bit into it with strong white teeth, brushing crumbs negligently on to the floor. 'The one irritation was that I got no dinner.'

'And?'

'Yes, I admit, this changes things. He have this girl with him? – this one the Germans were flapping about?'

'Yes.'

'Bit exaggerated all this, isn't it? I mean I don't know why you're after him, but when he sees you he grabs our heli. That's in itself not serious, is it? I mean there's no larcenous intent, so we're left with joyriding. Is a joyride in a heli any more dangerous or serious than the same thing in a sports car? But for him to do a thing like that makes me think there's more in this than meets the eye.'

Well, this Bratfisch might be casual, but he was not stupid.

'I don't know myself what he thinks I'm after. My instructions were to find him and learn why he chose to vanish from his home. He may have something on his mind I know nothing of. The point is that he feels himself cornered and he may do something more reckless than joyriding. He has a young girl with him who is innocent of anything at all.'

'Mm,' Bratfisch tapped the white teeth and hitched a bit of cheese out of some corner. 'We'd better go and look. And you must come, since you can recognize this chap. We've got no proper description. I may say I meant to sound lukewarm when you came to see me last night, because it all sounded a bit too hole-and-corner, and I hadn't had this chap signalled, or anything. Still – I can act on the signal Köln sent me about the girl. You do understand why I didn't regard that as serious? We had a smash and grab in a jeweller's last night, right here in the street. Impudence, that. It's been taking up most of the resources I possess. Still, we'll see what we can do now,' leading the way downstairs.

He had a car outside, one of the old BMW saloons that are extremely solid and a great deal faster than they look. 'Give me a description and I'll broadcast it,' he said with a finger flicked at the radio transmitter. 'Mark, this valley's not wide, and they may quite likely be still in it, since the roads are being watched. They left the heli at the head of the valley and skied down.'

*

After a bit of boy scout work they found the chalet where Marschal had been honeymooning with his tanzmariechen: there was nobody there. It was furnished with the ordinary things one finds in all mountain chalets. There were plenty of expensive things strewn about, from roses – flown into Innsbruck by plane at that time of year, and forced quite likely in Holland or Hyères, costing the earth – to a fancy Japanese camera which, alas, had no films in it. It was hard to say whether they had been back there or not. They had made little effort to take anything with them, and certainly no real luggage: the clothes that had been bought in München – and in Innsbruck! – were lying about everywhere. A careful search failed to turn up anything remarkable.

Back in Innsbruck a bit of hustling among files showed the chalet to be the property of an Italian business man: probably turn out to be a pal of Marschal's – and quite likely someone with something to do with the Sopex! Whether he had been there or not, there would be nothing suspect or unusual to him about Jean-Claude's turning up with a girl.

'They'll try to get out of Austria, now.'

'Well, there aren't all that many ways of getting out,' said Bratfisch comfortably. 'We've got the red Fiat, so they'd have to get another auto – and we've warned all garages and filling stations. Plane is right out, and I've got men on every train leaving Austria. He's got to follow the valleys and what choice does that give him? Back towards Salzburg, the other way into the Vorarlberg and over towards Constance, up towards Germany, Mittenwald and Garmisch, or south over the Brenner. That looks likeliest, with the place belonging to this whatsisname from Torino, but hell, it's easy enough to block the Brenner!'

'What about the high passes? He seems to be useful on skis.'

Bratfisch laughed.

'You don't know much about mountains, do you? First, there's an enormous amount of snow everywhere, and all but the main road passes are blocked. Second, there's a *föhn* blowing. Avalanche weather. Nobody with one penny's worth of sense is going to do any boy scout stuff on any mountains in these conditions, and anyone with no sense but a bad conscience would get stuck in a drift before he was up five hundred metres. Or might, very easily, get killed. This chap of yours wouldn't do anything like that. No, wait twenty-four hours and we have him in a bag, girl and all.'

Van der Valk, feeling slightly curious, passed the Kaisershof on his way back to supper. There was an uproarious party going on; the French ski-team, with a crowd of trainers and hangers-on from ski and wax manufacturers, as many journalists, and a good many of the Austrian equivalents, were having a whoopee for the end of the competition season. There had been a big prizegiving and speechmaking already, with a good many banalities from the burgomaster and the President of the International Federation, and the five National Federations, and the Alpine Club, and . . . Anne-Marie was gone. She had packed her skis on to her hired car, and driven off earlier that afternoon, the porter said. No, she had been alone. No, she had had no messages or telephone calls, nor had she made any. No, she had seemed quite calm and sunny.

It was easy enough to check. Anne-Marie, alone, yes, quite alone, yes, they were quite sure, had passed the border at Füssen half an hour ago, in the hired car still, with the skis on top. They had noticed her particularly – yes, naturally.

Where the hell was Füssen? He had heard of it – they had an ice hockey team there. After a minute's hunting on the map he found it, a little town just over the German border, thirty kilometres or so west of Garmisch. It didn't have to mean anything.

Anne-Marie had lost her taste for mountains and perhaps felt like a nice flat plain – Holland, for instance.

*

He couldn't sleep. He was overtired and overtense, and his shoulder was swollen, had stiffened, and was so painful that he could not lie on it. At midnight he was still wandering about Innsbruck. Competition skiers, whose batteries take a lot of recharging, sleep twelve hours when they can get it, but the season was over, and the revelry still in full blast. After months of being forbidden to drink, forbidden to smoke, forbidden to eat toffees, after months on a gloomy diet of grapefruit, raw carrots and underdone steak, the girls were letting down furiously. He wasn't surprised; they were kept as overwound as he was himself for months on end. He was in no mood for squeakers and balloons and dancing the surf; he found a little bar where he could do some nice neurotic solitary drinking.

There was Wien of course, a powerful magnet. But Jean-Claude could not know how seriously the Austrian police might be inclined to take people that jumped around in government helicopters – the most valuable tools of the mountain rescue brigades. A helicopter is a sacred cow in the Alps – there are too many places where the air is the only bridge between life and death.

There was Zürich; he was quite sure that the millionaire side of Marschal had not neglected to keep a few bolivars in Zürich – the town of Marshal Masséna!

Which way would the cat jump? Surely not Germany, with every bum policeman there looking for the tanzmariechen, and Heinz Stössel's highpowered machine. The Jugoslav and Czech and Hungarian borders appeared unlikely for obvious reasons: no, it must surely be Switzerland or Italy. And trains would be out, for Marschal would surely know that the passports on a train are easily checked if anyone cares to take the trouble. The answer lay on the roads, hiding on a lorry or something. Naturally, but he had to consider Marschal's character as well as those huge packets of banknotes: skulking like a refugee across the Curtain wasn't his style. He would find it more in his nature to try something impudent, a gay piece of bluff, the riskier the better: if he was caught, then it would be time to try a bribe. He could see Marschal sailing across the Italian frontier in a huge Rolls Royce, bowing slightly from side to side, with Ethiopian flags flying from the wings . . .

It was no use; he still couldn't sleep, even with half a bottle of brandy inside him. At four in the morning he was hunting again through the unsympathetic streets in search of humanity. Experience told him the only place he would find warmth was the railway station.

The humanity was only just out of bed, perfunctorily washed, and not talkative: a smell of damp clothes quarrelled with that of fresh bread and coffee. The man next door had a powerful agricultural flavour of mouldy hay about him, had disdained shaving, and had given himself early-morning courage by putting rum in his coffee. The *föhn* was blowing and a thick fog hung in the station. It was horribly cold, but not freezing; on the mountains thick wet nasty snow was drizzling down. The winter sports, he thought with relief, were over.

He had the prickling eyes and tender skin that come from not sleeping. His neighbour – how that damp loden coat smelt! – slept happily, waking miraculously at the exact moment his train came in: there, no doubt, he could have another little snooze between here and Salzburg, jolting to and fro with his mouth open in a sickly waft of rum.

Van der Valk smoked and meditated, the kind of philosophical meditation one does have on workmen's trains at five in the morning. It was still pitchblack out, blue and orange lights glaring livid through sleet, the mountains huge unguessable shapes brooding out there like statues on Easter Island. Van der Valk thought about passion.

There are two kinds, he was thinking. There is the northern kind, that thinks it is high on emotion and is only high on imagination. That is us: me, the Germans, the Scandinavians, the English, the Americans. Much given to misty unreality and sobbing gulping melodrama; we don't have passions, but we imagine them so strongly we delude ourselves that we are ready for any grand dramatic gesture. That is our romance, which is not romance at all, but romanticism. We weep buckets over passion, but we don't have it; we commit suicide all the time, and it is from pure self-pity. Our grand gestures are prompted by a moist and profuse sense of theatre.

Real passion belongs to Latin peoples. Read the newspaper in France or Italy. The crime of passion is a commonplace, whereas in Northern Europe it is extremely rare. For a man to shoot his wife, perhaps, and then himself, is a thing regarded as reasonable and psychologically probable. A man utterly lacking in imagination, a shop assistant, a traveller in chemical manure, will strangle his mistress, who has taken up with a sales-manager, walk into the local police station, and not cause even a lifted eyebrow.

One does not find the house of Bernarda Alba in Vancouver, thought Van der Valk. We can imagine it; a type like me, with an over-active imagination, will buy a toy cowboy-pistol and create a whole damn Mayerling in a suburban bedroom. Given a real pistol, we will flourish it about in a dramatic way, and if we have any normal intelligence we take good care the bullet goes into the bedroom ceiling.

The interesting people are those with mixed blood. Jean-Claude Marschal had streaks of northern blood, and could be misty, no doubt, with the best of them, and he had, quite undoubtedly, a strain of highly-coloured ancestry that was almost Corsican. He could be capable of a violent emotion. The tanzmariechen might be, to him, nothing but a good theatrical gesture – and she might be intensely real and very important; what the English governess was to the Duc de Choiseul-Praslin.

I am too much of a northerner, thought Van der Valk, with my veins full of Ibsen.

It must have been the dark, and the wet snow, and the unseen blind mountains, and a sound of horses outside of a sudden, and Austria, that made him think of Mayerling. Being a bad police-man, these events in classical tragedy had always interested him. Of course it is a gift to northern romanticism and the boulevard press. Royalty! It has everything. The long white gloves and the red roses, the gloomy hunting-lodge in the snow and the sound of waltzes in the Wiener Wald. High boots with spurs, and the clop-clop-creak of fiacres. Zither music, the soft chime of eighteenth-century clocks, and the echo of two revolver shots. Strip off all this goo, so dear to the heart of every North European, and what do you get? An obscure intrigue, that may have been political; was it in anybody's interest that the unstable Rudolf should not succeed the ancient, frugal, careful Franz-Josef on the Imperial throne?

That has to be stripped off too. It is fashionable nowadays to regard the last years of the Holy Roman Empire as the fall of the house of Usher. Doom, doom, doom. Waltzes play with infinite sadness through the echoing halls of Schönbrunn, the Papagenotor is wreathed in mist, a stinking miasma from the foul sluggish Danube, rank grass grows in the streets of Vienna, and the Hofburg is full of shrieking gibbering wraiths. The revolver shots of Mayerling echo at Sarajevo. We are far away from the Radetsky March on a snowy New Year's morning, Professor Willy conducting with the violin bow, a republican crowd. Happy New Year from the Wiener Filharmoniker.

We are even further from Baron Ochs, like Jupiter, happy in a thousand disguises, and the FeldMarschallin embodied in golden Lotte Lehmann. No, we are Richard Strauss, but not in Dresden in 1911. In the Dresden of 1945, looking at what a thousand English and American bombers did to the world's most beautiful city, packed with refugees, where there was not one single object of military importance.

Thinking of Mayerling, one must forget all that. There remains nothing but a man and a girl.

The interesting thing is surely that at this distance one cannot really know whether one reads the signs right. From the north, of course, it is as plain as print: a nervous and hysterical prince of weak character who may or may not have become entangled in politics, who killed his mistress and himself in a theatrical gesture.

But we do not know. Rudolf had dark, sudden, ancient blood; there is no family in history to which mystery attaches as much as to the house of Hapsburg. Think of Marie Antoinette's necklace, of the Prisoner of the Temple, of Don Carlos and Antonio Perez, of General Weygand's parentage: think of the blood shed to keep them on their throne – one example, the English blood that painted the slaughterhouse of Malplaquet.

Van der Valk did not know much about the little baroness of sixteen either – Marie Vetsera. She might have had a strong character. It wasn't even an Austrian name, he thought; what part of the empire had she come from? Hungary, perhaps, or Austrian Poland. He was a bad policeman, but too experienced to make up his mind in a hurry about what happened at Mayerling, and too experienced a man to be northern and denounce the passion of a man of forty for a girl of sixteen as ridiculous. It might, after all, have been a crime of pure passion, as real as that of a Marseillais soap-salesman and a shop assistant from Nevers (Prisunic, Grands Boulevards, imitation-leather-handbags counter) in a furnished room in Kremlin-Bicêtre.

He sighed. That was what happened when you had no sleep, and went to drink coffee after too much cognac at the Station Buffet at four in the morning. Come now. Sixteen-year-old girls no longer think like Marie Vetsera. They chew gum, dream of meeting a pop singer on the ski-slope, and have names like Schwiewelbein.

He thought about his wife. Arlette. She looked northern enough, large, blonde, a scrap over-ripe in the figure. But the time or two he had seen Arlette in a red rage he knew very well that her emotions were not to be trifled with: she was not theatrical, she could not be trusted to think whereabouts the bullet ought to land before she pulled the trigger, and if she got up on any barricade there would be no idiotic North-European far-far-better-thinging. He reeled off back to bed and fell instantly asleep.

*

He woke at midday, and felt like being a detective. He was going to have a good dinner, and shake the ghosts off, think about his immediate problem: if Jean-Claude Marschal wanted to get out of Austria, how would he go about it?

There was a very good delicate sauerbraten, with almonds and raisins in it, not too vinegary. There were nice feathery mashed potatoes, and there was red cabbage with a very faint flavour of cinnamon . . . He felt a great deal better. A good many tourists had left, and the hotel staff, with the end of the season in sight, were feeling lighthearted.

They could have mixed with a crowd of tourists. It was possible and indeed had been done often enough, since nobody ever looked at tourists' passports; the most was to count and see if the number came out right . . . But those busloads were too obvious, and too many people would know, and the frontiers would not be quite as perfunctory as usual . . . Was there any other group where a person more or less, even two, would pass unnoticed? He dropped his napkin, bent to pick it up, and was unpleasantly reminded of a hard bumpy ski-slope and his bruised tender shoulder.

Those gangs of skiers that had been making such an uproar in the Kaisershof last night . . . There were crowds of characters that nobody thought about, accompanying a ski-team. Families and friends, hangers-on, as well as the technical boys, timekeepers and whatnot and the little man that measured the humidity of the snow. Jean-Claude had once been a competition skier. He ran to the police bureau. Bratfisch was not there, but he found another character.

'How do the ski-teams travel? In a block, or do they scatter?'

'I suppose they just dribble off home by car in bits and scraps. The French have a whole gang – the caravan as usual. Twenty or thirty autos, and of course their bus.'

'Bus?'

'They shovel all their material, the skis and so on, into an ordinary touring bus. Handiest way of getting it all around. Stays with them through the season.'

'Which way did they go? Home, I know, but which way?'

'Shortest way, I suppose – over the Arlberg, turn down towards the St Gotthard, Furka valley, Rhône valley, straight through to France.'

'Raise the Feldkirch frontier station on the phone for me, will you?'

Yes, the caravan had passed. Check the passports? Good grief, they were all piled like corpses after the big party. Why bother? Everybody knew the ski-team; it spent half the year toing and froing between one end of the Alps and the other.

Switzerland confirmed that nobody would bother checking such well known passport photographs, and Van der Valk felt he was getting warm. It was too late, evidently; they were all back in dear old Chamonix by now. They had eaten at Andermatt, gay and in obstreperous holiday mood once woken up. The Swiss, more literal-minded than the Austrian, had a detail or two to add. There had been two caravans really, another row of twelve or fifteen autos after the first. What? Yes, of course; journalists, photographers, and the French radio commentators.

'Yes, of course.' The ski-team was followed by its attendant circus of sports journalists, and that was another crowd that would be familiar to Mr Marschal. Indeed, now that he thought of it . . . ski competitors, managers and trainers followed one another in quick tempo – no results, no contract – whereas these specialized journalists had often covered the same big meetings for twenty years – and those tatty passports were as familiar to every frontier guard in the Alps as Sir Arnold Lunn's. It was so damn easy that he knew immediately that Marschal would have loved the notion, which had just the simplicity and impudence that appealed: no nerve-wracking creeping round Germany or Switzerland; one fell asleep in Austria and woke up in Chamonix as fresh as though one had gone straight through by the Arlberg Express.

What did he risk? Van der Valk took the night train, and stepped out himself in the sharp bright morning in Chamonix, where there was a station buffet with only a slightly different smell to the one in Innsbruck, and coffee only a scrap blacker and more bitter. He missed the fleshpots of Austria a bit, and gluttonously put first butter and then apricot jam on a huge piece of brioche. It was too early in the morning to go running about, so he sat comfortably in the warmth and had two cigarettes and some more coffee, and read the *Figaro* of the day before, with its report from a 'special correspondent in Innsbruck' . . . He walked out into a blinding piercing brilliant morning and took his hat off to the majestic, faintly boring silhouette of the Mont Blanc.

*

An hour after a visit to the Chamber of Commerce he was in a street on the outskirts of the town, a very French street leading up a hillside to nowhere, made of gravel for drainage, the potholes and bumps nicely levelled with snow, and people's furnace clinker strewn about to keep it from getting too slidy. The Impasse des Roses, the roses were in people's front gardens, covered with little plastic sacks against frost.

The houses were French too, amusing and individual. Ridiculous mixtures of the Savoyard chalet, made of logs built out over the hillsides, and fantasies of prestressed concrete, with garages in the basement instead of cows. They all had glassed terraces and double windows, eccentric roofs, tremendous rockgardens and the kind of letterbox with a wooden bird of no known species that nods its beak when you shove an electricity bill in the slot.

The house he was looking for had a wrought-iron gate, crazy pavements, and a gothic front door. Outside the garage, where a vertiginous ramp dived into the earth's stressed-concrete bowels, a green Peugeot 404 was parked in a nosedive like a stuka. It was quite new-looking but much travel-stained; Van der Valk regarded it with affection. An aluminium plaque said 'Serailler, Journalist': he rang the bell.

'I've an idea he's still asleep but it's high time he got up anyway. Who shall I say? OK.' He could be a policeman from Amsterdam or from Timbuctoo; it was all in the day's work and left a journalist's wife indifferent. He was put in the living-room, offered a cigarette, and given time to look about.

Plenty of the usual paraphernalia – table with typewriter, shelves full of directories and reference dictionaries, rows of files with photos and cuttings, a tape recorder on the phone-table and an Italian majolica jar full of pencils. The big sunny room was untidy with souvenir dollies, more and more outrageous ashtrays, stuffed animals, and ski-ing trophies: there was a large and amazingly miscellaneous collection of books, and Van der Valk was glad he had come. Mr Serailler looked like an amusing person. He was saved further speculation by the door opening and the man himself appearing, no more bothered by the police at nine in the morning than his wife had been.

A muscular forty-five, with a splendid mountain tan and the characteristic long fine wrinkles at the eyes. Short hair gone grey early, still wet from a comb held under the tap and run through it. Tight blue trousers that looked like denim but had cost a lot more money; a Mégève sweater whose sleeves he had tucked up above the elbows and which had a little spatter of toothpaste on the front. Hand-knitted socks and no shoes. He padded over the smooth wooden floor and shook hands amiably.

'Really was high time I got out of bed.'

'Just back from Innsbruck?'

'That's it. Long drive but the roads weren't bad. What can I do for you?'

'You've been around the circuit a good few years – not many people you don't know.'

'Suppose not. Know most of them too well. Used to be a skier myself, but never all that good. Never got out of the business.'

'Ever come across a man named Marschal?'

'Probably, common name enough. Skier?'

'Playboy style but pretty good I believe. Ten years ago or more like fifteen, might have been in the top twenty.'

'Of course. Jean-Claude. Was fifth at Kitzbühel once when I was seventh. Well, well. Sure I remember. Didn't practise enough, like so many more. Might have been a champion otherwise. Wonder what happened to him? Had lots of money – no need to work for his living like us.'

The story had gone on too long; Van der Valk smiled a bit, secretly. It was all a little too casual.

'He was in Innsbruck last week.'

'You don't say. Wonder why I didn't run into him.'

'He was in Chamonix yesterday.'

'Well well. Old stamping ground. Nostalgic pilgrimage, perhaps. Why the interest?' It was too casual; there was no doubt about it.

'I just wondered whether it was you that gave him the lift.'

The journalist did not change his easy smile. He felt in his trouser pocket, brought out a pair of horn-rimmed glasses, and put them on his nose, from where he pushed them up on his forehead like snowgoggles. Gentian-blue eyes looked at Van der Valk curiously.

'Whose business is it that you're making your business? – I'm not quite clear. Mine?'

'No, his. I want to see him. I guessed he'd hitched a lift with the caravan.'

'Is there anything illegal about that?'

'I'm just catching up, or trying to, without getting out of breath.'

'What goes on? You say you're from the police. He hasn't paid a parking fine or something?'

'Oh, nobody's worried about that helicopter.'

A broad grin appeared.

'You don't tell me it was Jean-Claude that pinched the helicopter? Ha – just like him.' Bark of laughter. 'Hardly an extraditable offence, though.'

'You got children?'

'One,' startled. 'Girl of twelve. Why?'

'Does she ski?'

'Sure. I'm sorry, you know, but I don't get any of this.'

'Suppose your girl had gone to Innsbruck, say, and was suddenly missing. Nowhere to be seen. What would you do?'

'I know nothing about any girl missing.'

'But that girl with Jean-Claude is missing, for all that. Her parents are terribly worried – would you blame them?'

'Of course not, but I don't see what all this has to do with me.'

'Simply that if you'd known you might not have been so quick to agree.'

'Agree to what?'

'Giving Jean-Claude a lift. He must have said he wished to avoid anything looking like police. The frontier guards, for instance.'

'Who said anything about my giving Jean-Claude or any girl a lift?'

'Ach man, don't be childish. I don't care whether you did or not. You couldn't have known about anything serious. Quite likely he said the Austrian police were narked with him about the helicopter. But you were all together. If you gave him the lift someone else will have noticed it, and if someone else did you would have noticed it. Just tell me straight out and save everybody trouble.'

The wife came in and dumped coffee on the table in front of Serailler. He sat down with his eyebrows knitted and stirred thoughtfully.

'Want some?'

'No thanks, I had some at the station.'

'Look. Jean-Claude is an old friend. We used to compete together. Once I was third in the national champs and he was fourth, only one point behind me. I gave him and his friend a lift – you can find that out easily enough, I suppose. And further than that I've nothing to say, not without rather better reasons than you've given me so far.'

'Why d'you think he pinched the helicopter?'

'In the years when I knew him he was a wild boy. Doing something like that wouldn't be unlike him. I never gave it a thought.'

'One does things like that at twenty. One doesn't do them at forty.'

'That's true.'

'It surprised me. I'll tell you frankly, there is something in all this that may be serious.'

'You mean the girl?'

'I mean him. The girl's disappearance isn't particularly serious. It could be made out technically to look like a crime, but there's nothing to show he offered her any violence or did anything vicious with her. There's more to it. The man is missing from his home and there's nothing to show why. Why does he vanish from his own home and persuade some girl to vanish from hers? How well do you know him?'

'Like you say, fifteen years ago – hell, it's nearer twenty – I knew him pretty well. I've seen him since a couple of times winter-sporting. Didn't he marry a girl that was a skier too? Belgian girl – I've forgotten her name.'

'Yes. Did you ever see anything in him out of the ordinary?'

'Everybody's out of the ordinary if you look deep enough,' dry.

'Sure. How was he on the road?'

'Ordinary. Nothing unusual. We hardly talked though. While I was driving he was asleep, and when he drove it was my turn. We'd both been at the party.' Dear lord, thought Van der Valk: he was under my nose there the whole time. 'Said he'd been doing some ski-ing, said he was pretty tired, said he had no auto and would I give him a lift home? I agreed, naturally.'

'The girl?'

'She was very quiet. To be honest I hardly noticed her. They were very affectionate with each other. Jean-Claude was gay and happy.'

'Maybe because he was being clever and doing something exciting. The police of three countries are looking for him. I was looking for him in Holland, the German police are looking for their girl and know she's with him, and the Austrians aren't bothered much about their helicopter but would like to kick his arse for him. All the frontier posts were after him.'

'I had no idea . . . I was driving. I just showed the auto papers and my pass. They know us all, of course.'

'That was just what he was counting on.'

'I'll be damned.'

'Where did he go?'

'I asked him back here. He said no, he was going to catch a train.'

'Where would the train be going, that hour?'

'Besançon and points north.'

'You know where he was headed for?'

The gentian-blue eyes looked at Van der Valk for a long time before Serailler answered. Van der Valk hoped he would answer, because he hadn't any way of making him.

'I have an idea,' slowly, 'that he has a cottage or something in the Vosges.'

'Know the address?'

'No.'

'Phone number?'

'There isn't any phone.'

'Whereabouts is it?'

'Fraid I don't know.'

Van der Valk gave him the big homely grin.

'How d'you know there's no phone then.'

'You think he's a bit off the rails, do you?' suddenly.

'I don't know any damn thing. I'm a bit worried though. I'd like to see this girl's parents knowing she was safe and happy. I'd like to talk to Marschal. There's nothing criminal against him. I'm not going to arrest him or anything. He has a right to leave home any time he wishes. But there are other people involved. He left his wife – she's anxious. He left his job – they're anxious. Obviously you thought it all a scrap queer too or you wouldn't have been so leery of me. It's better that you tell me.'

'I have the phone number of a café,' said Serailler slowly. 'He said they could give him a message.'

'He hasn't called you.'

'No.'

'But he gave you the number to call in case anybody came nosing round here after him.'

'I guess so,' said Serailler a little unhappily.

'You see? Don't call the number – it might make things a lot worse. You notice I'm not threatening you with anything, but if a criminal charge ever came out of this and the lawyers discovered that you'd helped him twice, once after I'd warned you, they might take a dim view. That's just a friendly remark.'

Serailler got up, walked over to his table, and picked a note-book out of a drawer. He fluttered the leaves, tore one out, did not look at it further, walked back, and gave it to Van der Valk.

'There you are. You may be right. I don't know what it is nor where it is. What you do with it's your affair. Jean-Claude can't

complain I've shopped him. He should have told me I was taking a·
risk in taking him over the border.'

'What did the guard say at the frontier?'

'He asked who they were, and I just said two friends, of course,
and did he want me to give them a poke, and he just laughed and said
let the sleepers sleep, as long as I knew them it was all right.'

'If he had woken them up you'd have been carrying the ball.'

'That's what has occurred to me. I forget it again, because that's
for a friend, but I'm not dipping myself any further.'

*

The telephone number was written hurriedly, slantwise, the way
one might while holding the paper across the steering wheel while
sitting in an auto. Somewhere in the Vosges . . . He went to the
post office with it, for French telephone numbers depend on a
system of numeral prefixes that are a trap to the unwary, since they
are sometimes, but by no means always, the same as the depart-
mental numerals on auto plates . . .

Half an hour later he was in a café, drinking gentian: like
Maigret he had got stuck on the same drink. It was a good choice,
he thought, because it is a mountain drink, and this is a mountain
story. He had bought the Michelin map of the Vosges, and after a
bit of searching he found the village, tucked up in the foothills,
between the high ground and the Alsace plain, not far from
Saverne and the pass of the Zorn. It would be nice there, he
thought; the Vosges get steadily lower as one goes north, and
indeed beyond the Zorn there is nothing above six hundred metres:
one is well away from the picturesque tourist country and the wine
district, and the over-closely bunched villages of the plain have
straggled out into the beech and pine woods and the short slippery
grass.

It would be characteristic, of course, of Marschal to have a
hideout and for it to be in a place like that. He could easily believe
that the man had even kept it secret from his wife. He might have
had it some time, perhaps years. A typical piece of northern
romanticism, that, in keeping with the Napoleonic bank accounts

and the rest of this boy scout side to Marschal's nature. Well, the man had a right to do it. It would be a pleasant antidote to Canisius, and the Sopex, and public relations, and maybe to Anne-Marie as well. No, he wasn't going to phone Canisius; there were altogether too many things he didn't know. The part Canisius had played in this was obscure; he felt almost ready to bet that Canisius had known – or at least guessed – a lot more of what Jean-Claude was up to than he had told the police.

The train north from Chamonix to Strasbourg is a longish ride, but not dull, since the Alps give way to the Jura, and the Jura to the Belfort gap, and from Belfort onwards there are the Vosges on one's left, and Van der Valk, watching the sunset, felt peaceful. It was all a lot of much-ado-about-nothing when all was said. If Mr Marschal had not had a great deal of money it would have been both more difficult and less of a holiday, but the money had left a blazed trail, and he had had an amusing ride about the Alps, and what did it all amount to? A neurotic man with too much money, at once too old and too young for his age, who had never been in want or need, who had never learned the lessons of tenacity and patience that are learned by having to fight for one's footing: a poor chap. If he had had no money he would be pathetic and if he had too much it was equally pathetic. It wasn't anything to get hysterical about; he would catch up with the fellow here at his little hideaway, and give him a talking to, and get this girl back, and what Marschal did then was his affair. Let Canisius worry about that: it wasn't police business. He had something to eat, and got a rather squashed suit out of his case, for he was still in mountain fancy-dress, and settled down to read the book he had bought, Albert Simonin's *Paws off the Cake*, which is extremely amusing because it is written in gangster slang, and passed happy hours trying to imagine how Raymond Chandler would have put it into American.

It was evening, and dusk on a chilly March evening, in Strasbourg. He had never been there, and had a peaceful walk to taste the atmosphere, which he liked very much. Pity he would not be staying; he would have enjoyed a few days here. No, he had had

94

enough running around. He was in the mood to go home, to taste again the flavour of his own house, to hear the tones of his wife's voice, to eat familiar food, look with love at familiar objects, tell himself he was home, and that next day he would get up and bicycle as usual to police headquarters. He had really had enough of mountains, and picturesque scenery, and the sharp delicate pleasure of watching a top-class girl skier slaloming. He had a fairly unexciting dinner in an unexciting hotel near the station, and phoned Arlette before going virtuously to bed.

'I'm in Strasbourg. Nice, here: we'll go together some time.'

'You're getting around, aren't you? How's the ski-ing coming along?'

'Shut up about the ski-ing; my shoulder still hurts. There's nothing at the moment I want to see more than Amsterdam on a rainy day. Nice and flat!'

'When d'you think you'll be home?'

'I might get finished tomorrow with any luck. Storm in a teacup. Just that this fellow I'm supposed to be hunting for runs round like a rabbit. I've found out where the hole is, now. I'll have a scené with this girl, no doubt, but that's only to be expected. All this has given me a strong taste for domesticity. You all right?'

'Yes, but getting sick as well of being widowed.'

'Ha. I'll ring you tomorrow: I ought to know something by then.'

*

It was different again next morning; wet snow was falling heavily. It was not sticking on the streets of Strasbourg, but he had had enough of snow. He did not put on his suit, but the serge trousers and the canadienne jacket he had bought – on expenses – in Innsbruck, and the mountain boots, and the sweater Anne-Marie had bought. It brought him back with a jolt. Why had Anne-Marie tried to seduce him? Why had she given that shriek of warning to Jean-Claude? He had passed it off as a whim of a spoiled woman who is too rich and can indulge her caprice. He stamped out rather ruffled after his dreams of peace from the day before, not so sure that he was done with mountains, and rented a car, which was a bitch like all rented cars. The gearbox was anything but sweet, the visibility was lousy, the heating was too hot, as it always is, he made several false turnings – no, he had to clamp the teeth of patience on the bullet of chagrin still.

He could not see the Vosges through the drizzling mass of low cloud, till he was right on top of them. They were only hills here. He lurched up a narrow foothill road off the auto-route, and found his village, no more than a cluster round the four angles of a crossroad, a Romanesque church, a school, a real French country *mairie* with grandiose pillars outside to support the dignity of the Republic.

The café whose telephone number had been written on a scrap of paper in Chamonix was no trouble either. There it was with farm buildings clumped behind it, and inside a powerful French rural smell a hundred years old. Polished pitchpine, and a tiled floor scrubbed with *eau-de-Javel*. Straw, denim overalls, and dog, white wine and vegetable soup, onions, smoked bacon, and ironing. As usual, there was the mixture of the very old and the very new: that dented zinc certainly dated from Napoleon the Third, and the espresso machine that glittered with chrome and little magic handles and winking red lights standing alongside . . . A huge television set, gaudy as only the French make them, was flanked by classic decorative themes: a large china shepherd dog and a stuffed otter with a stuffed trout in his mouth. There was a beefy man drinking vino, in blue overalls, a thin man in a cap, and a stringy woman peeling carrots.

'Good morning.'

'Moyng,' came a triple grunt.

At this Van der Valk knew it would be difficult. There are two kinds of French people, the nice ones and the sour ones. The sour ones can generally be melted, but it is sometimes hard work. Out of three pairs of eyes looked the glummest kind of peasant distrust.

'Soup smells good.'

'Ugh.'

'Gentian.' It had become a habit. The man with the cap had to go to the cellar to hunt for a fresh bottle, which he did with poor grace, as though it were an unheard-of demand on his time and energy.

'Have one with me.'

'I'll take a glass of white,' in a grudging mutter. The beefy man and the stringy woman seemed to be having an argument. It might have been something to do with potatoes, but the patois they talked was enigmatic. There were French words in it, and words that sounded like German, and an intonation sounding rather like Welsh. He couldn't be certain they were talking about potatoes, but he knew the way all peasants have of sounding furiously angry while really remaining on quite amicable terms.

'I'm looking for Mr Marschal.'

'Who's that?'

'He lives here.'

'Joh.'

'Far?'

'Ugh.'

'In the village?'

'Up the road.'

'Not far, then?'

'Joh.'

'I'll go and knock him up if you'll point me the road out.'

'Nobody there.'

Oh, god, thought Van der Valk; not again.

'Joh,' said the woman suddenly. 'Is too.'

'What?'

'Someone there.'

'Ugh. Gone.'

'Shutters were up yesterday.'

'Down today,' said the thin man with relish.

'I can always try,' offered Van der Valk. 'Have another glass?'

'Joh.'

The beefy man, who had been turning his empty glass round and round and gazing absorbed at the blank television screen, now took a hand.

'Isn't, neither. Auto's there.'

'Have one too,' said Van der Valk hospitably. 'What about you, Madame?'

'Ugh. Give me a sour stomach.'

'Spot of prunelle?'

'Joh.'

This was perhaps the key with which Shakespeare unlocked his heart, thought Van der Valk, who was beginning to feel slightly drunk amid all this nonsense. The woman thawed suddenly. 'You show'm th'way, Albert.'

Albert seemed to be the beefy one. He was not at all easy to detach from his glass, but after taking off his beret twice to scratch, unwinding his scarf and putting it back again, and accepting one of Van der Valk's cigarettes, he got unstuck.

Albert had a tractor outside. He climbed into the saddle, pointed up the side street with a finger like an aubergine, and said, 'Can't miss'm. Got green shutters.'

Van der Valk felt there were twenty houses at least with green shutters.

'Red house,' Albert admitted, and turned the starter key.

There was a house built of the Vosges sandstone, and it did have green shutters, and they were down. It was not the isolated log-cabin of fantasy, but a perfectly ordinary house in a village street, standing alone but elbowed in on by bigger neighbours. There was a stone wall with house-leeks growing on it, and a wooden door on the paint of which the village children had written obscenities. Along the wall was a wider double door, through which nobody had passed today, he thought, for the wet snow was untouched.

Inside the smaller door, which gave to his hand, no one had been either – not for some hours, at least, though that was not much help. The house was set cornerwise towards the street, with a tiny first floor balcony built out across the angle; it was a small house, but old, and remarkably solid. There was an oak front door with a narrow curtained porch window. He disregarded this for the moment and followed the wide paved path that led round to the back. Here was a sort of little yard, with an old-fashioned French wash-house and an open shed, in which were several empty wine bottles, a pile of kindling wood, and a dustbin. The back door led obviously to the kitchen.

There was no sign of any activity, but between the door and the shed stood an expensive auto, a black Lancia saloon, two and a half litre. The showroom polish was still on it under the thin layer of snow, and the label of the Strasbourg garage was untarnished: Van der Valk had to grin a little. That Jean-Claude – he bought new cars and left them lying about the way you or I leave a half-empty box of matches. He tapped on the door of the kitchen – the shutters were down inside. Nothing happened. He frowned, and tried the kitchen door. It yielded, and he frowned some more. He got down on a cold, wet, snowy step, squirmed with his hand, got the bottom of the shutter off the floor, and wriggled under it, not at all an easy job. It made a hell of a noise but nobody came to inquire what he might think he was doing. He didn't like all this a bit.

It was perhaps the extreme ordinariness of the house that struck one most. It might have been any suburban kitchen he was stand-ing in, with its very ordinary gas-stove, refrigerator, whitewood cupboards faced with Formica and table to match. Everything was neat and tidy and, as far as he could see, clean. There was still some soup in a pot on the stove, onions in a metal rack. In the fridge was meat and milk, an opened packet of butter, half a tin of tomato purée, a few slices of ham still in greaseproof paper, a plastic box half full of grated cheese. It was like a million French homes where the wife has gone to work as well as the husband; the house seems dead and empty, but will come to life again suddenly at six that evening.

The only difference was that this house was cold. He looked at the radiator – its tap was turned on.

In the hall was a cupboard with a pierced back for ventilation, through to the front porch, and a wiremesh front. It held a whole camembert and a piece of roquefort.

He did not go at once into either of the downstairs rooms, but down to the cellar. Everything here too had a look of reassuring permanence, of a house lived in for many years, kept by a careful housewife. Nothing could give one more the feeling of stability and a peaceful, patterned, regulated life than these brooms and dusters, these tins of paint and polish, these bottles of turpentine and caustic soda and *eau-de-Javel*, the vacuum cleaner hanging in its place and the shoe brushes in their tin. There was even a solid carpenter's table with a backboard and tools hanging on nails. It was the basement of an elderly couple whose children are grown up, who own their house and have a little money in the bank, who grow some vegetables in the garden and keep a few chickens. An ex-foreman in the Post Office or on the railways, who likes fishing and taking his gun out now and again after a rabbit, proud of his tomato plants and his dahlias, who has a couple of bottles of good wine and a box of cigars put away for when his son-in-law comes at the New Year and the Toussaint, who is to be found in the local café every evening between six and seven for two pernods and a game of belote.

Not the house of Jean-Claude Marschal.

Van der Valk went through to the back basement and the coal-cellar. A good half-ton of coke was piled under the chute, and there was wood chopped alongside an old stump scarred with axecuts. Old packing cases stacked for kindling; a pile of neatly sawed logs, another pile of yellowing *Couriers d'Alsace*; the floor was swept with a kitchen broom that stood in its appointed place next to the axe, and a one-man crosscut saw hung where it should on two rusty nails. It was all so perfect that he had a rush of aching home-sickness at the peace and order of it all.

The furnace was very slightly warm. He opened the door. It had not been raked and was full of ash; he felt the ash with his hand and drew the hand back quickly: grey and dead as it looked it was still holding heat. That furnace had been stoked anyway inside fifteen hours; it was the type one makes up twice a day. Van der Valk trudged back up to street level.

Silence and a little dust lay on the polished furniture, faded cheap carpets lay on the polished floorboards, everything was old fashioned, provincial and ugly. An ornate radio had a vase of flowers standing on it: the flowers were still fresh. On one corner was a dresser with a glass front; here Mother had kept the good plates for visitors, the liqueur glasses, and the souvenirs brought home by soldier sons from Indo-China. They were gone. In their place stood six porcelain figures. Van der Valk opened the door and took one out to handle it: he did not know much about such things, but he knew that this was Dresden work from the best period. That marquis dancing, that coquettish and sophisticated shepherd-girl cuddling a monkey, that splendid parrot – those could be by Kändler. And those were not acquired by an ex-foreman on the SNCF – those came from Jean-Claude. In which case they were quite certainly Kändler, and worth at a guess five hundred pounds apiece.

He tried the other room. Ah . . . Jean-Claude had been here. There was a piece bought from an antique dealer – yes, when he looked more closely all these pieces had been bought from the kind of provincial dealer that specializes in ancient farmhouse and peasant furnishings and sells them to filmstars from Paris who wish to give their country houses an authentic look. Authenticity from the fifteenth and sixteenth centuries, as this was, costs many millions. There was a sort of window-seat that gleamed like water with age and loving handling. The wood was dark and had violent unexpected swirls and courses in it of a sort of burnt orange that had been yellow three hundred years before. What could it be? Perhaps box? He had no notion. On it stood a different kind of collection, to which Van der Valk got down on his knees. Stones. Precious stones mounted on little socles of wood, of bronze, of iron, of crystal. Opal matrix, rough turquoise, raw emerald. He had no idea of the names; the geologist distinguishes hundreds and can recognize the provenance of each, for these brilliant colours and exquisite shapes have each their individual unique home. That delicate rose pink is from the Urals and that peacock green from the Canadian Rockies, that amarynth quartz is only found in St

Helena and that amazing dark red came from the volcanoes of the Puy de Dôme. Amethysts from Brazil and jade from Tibet; rock crystal more precious than its weight in uncut diamond, and opal eggs that are made by upland Indians on the Paraguay border. The beryl and the sardonyx, the ruby and the chrysoprase . . .

They had not only been kept dusted: they had been picked up and loved and handled. They had been felt by the toes of Greek sponge-fishers, stroked the throat of a seven-year-old girl, been contoured by blind men's fingers, played with by mandarin emperors and little Egyptian boys with bare bottoms and ophthalmia. That one had passed from a Congo pygmy with sleeping sickness to a colonial administrator with blackwater, had been brought to France by a syphilitic German Legionary to bed down in the chalk of arthritic fingers under the arcades of the Palais Royal. No dirt, no vileness, no meanness, no sickness could touch its beauty and purity. Poor Jean-Claude.

Van der Valk straightened up with a sigh. In the hall there was a rifle on one of those ornate weapon stands beloved of French hunters, all fake St Hubert, with antlers and carved wood. He looked at it incuriously; it was time to go upstairs. The wide shallow stairs of polished oak creaked under his feet, and he had the absurd shame one always has at making too much noise. The rifle was a much heavier calibre than one finds usually in people's houses, he thought vaguely: every Frenchman that lives in the country keeps a .22 for rats, cats, hooded crows and the fox he always suspects may be after the chickens – but that was the kind of thing one took to shoot lions with.

Light came through the wooden shutters in thin splinters and gave a dim unreal look to the bedroom. But there were two people in the big bed, real enough, even if they were dead. There was still a tiny trace of the sharp scent that stings the inside of the nose, which comes from two copper-jacket seven-sixty-five pistol cartridges. Mayerling . . .

He had to go and find the gendarmerie, he would have to explain who he was and what he was doing, they would have to call the lieutenant – he supposed there would be one in Saverne – and he,

102

after listening to Van der Valk's ridiculous tale that went on half an hour too long, would very likely decide he would have to ring Strasbourg, making faces at the idea of Authority, possibly even Paris, come to make faces in their turn in his own district.

*

It all went off exactly as he had suspected. While they were waiting for the lieutenant of the gendarmerie, the doctor, the magistrate, the technical men, and the ambulance, Van der Valk sat in the downstairs room with the precious stones in them. There were three or four books scattered about: paperback thrillers of the Série Noire type which he did not even glance at, a cheap edition of the poems of Baudelaire. Yes, he could quite see that; Baudelaire was the kind of person that would appeal to Jean-Claude Marschal. He had largely forgotten the poems, they had never appealed to him. Wasn't it Sartre who called Baudelaire a deliberate failure, who had chosen a bad conscience, chosen to feel guilty, chosen sterility? Not that he cared much for Sartre! but these particular remarks had always seemed to him like sound sense: the fact was that the fellow had been a drip. Not altogether his own fault – Sartre had exaggerated, of course, sympathy with people he didn't approve of not being his strongest point. Van der Valk started to read the poems; he had nothing else to do. Thinking would come later. This was not a thinking time; this was the bureaucratic time-lapse between pressing the button and getting an answer.

Spleen – now how did one translate spleen? Depression? – too weak. Ennui? – too vague. Manic depression – too forcible and too clinical. He was sure the Germans had a good compound abstract, five syllables long, meaning black-self-disgust-Supposed in-medieval-times-to-be-governed-by-internal-organ. Spleen was untranslatable. The answer was that it didn't need translating; everybody understood it.

He read the poem with a fresh eye; he hadn't had it under his eye in years. It was a lot better than he had thought it.

'I am like the king of a rainy country: rich – and impotent: young – and very old. Who despises the bowing-down of his

103

preceptors, is as bored with his dogs as with all his other creatures, whom nothing now, neither game nor falcon, can cheer. Not even subjects come to die beneath his balcony. A grotesque song from the indulged clown can no longer unwrinkle the forehead of this cruelly ill man: his fleurdelysed bed has become a tomb, and the ladies in waiting, who find any prince good looking, can think up no more lewd costumes to drag a smile from this young skeleton. The expert that makes his gold has never managed to purify the corrupt element in his being, and in the bloodbaths the Romans showed us, recalled to their memory by ageing tyrants, he has failed to rewarm the dulled stupor of a corpse in which blood no longer flows, but Lethe's green water.'

The lieutenant of gendarmerie had read Baudelaire, perhaps, but had other things to think about, and no time at the present moment for poems. (It turned out later that at his office desk, when he had spare time, he read Pascal.) Since this was his district, he was mostly interested in what these people were doing here. There wasn't much he could do about the two in the bed; they were dead, and there was nothing the police could do to help that, was there? He found a few stray facts to go on in the village: Mr Marschal, pronounced like Marchal, a common name anywhere in France, had owned this house for five years or more, bought it after the old couple had died, from a nephew in Paris with no interest in a house in some Vosges village he had never heard of. Mr Marschal had not come here often, seven or eight times a year, perhaps; mostly for two or three days only; always alone; longest anybody remembered his staying was a fortnight. Nobody had bothered about this; the world was full of eccentric people that left their houses empty. An old woman in the village had had the keys. She had been very well paid to go there every second day or so, to keep things clean and in order. She was accustomed to light the stove once a week to get the place dry and aired.

Yes, she had seen him arrive with a young girl. No, that hadn't struck her. She had always thought he would turn up with a woman sooner or later. No, he had been laughing and joking. Not

104

depressed-seeming a bit, if you asked her. Like a couple in love rather than a couple having a furtive week-end.

*

The lieutenant was not happy with Van der Valk. This rigmarole of millionaires and winter sports had really nothing to do with him, he conveyed. There might be something odd about it, he agreed, but that was for Strasbourg to decide. A double death had taken place on his territory, straightforward suicide pact, and he had a lot of forms to fill in. He thought that Van der Valk had better repeat his tale to the criminal divisionnaire in Strasbourg.

Police headquarters in Strasbourg is in a street with a gentle, innocent name. The Street of the Blue Cloud. It has a narrow, heavy frontage, imitation classic, and an archway where uniformed agents stand around bored scratching themselves with sub-machine-guns. They do not look in the least brutal or sinister; kindly, thickset, family men with corns and five o'clock shadow who do difficult and unpleasant work with good humour and get paid little enough for it.

Inside there is a cobbled eighteenth-century courtyard with radio vans and squad cars parked, and the sober black Peugeots of senior officers. Beyond the courtyard is a big building with a monstrous chill double staircase upon which the most fairy of police feet falls like a rifle-shot. Van der Valk gave all this a professionally appreciative look and decided that it was even dingier than the Prinsengracht in Amsterdam, but a great deal gayer. He was directed on his way by a good-humoured old-China-hand that had thirty years on the cops and still nothing wrong with his digestion: a young agent in the hall was doing an imitation of his superior officer for the benefit of two more with a good deal of schoolboy laughter, and the plainclothes man upstairs, walking between room three-oh-four and three-seventy with an armful of files, was whistling '*Vissi d'arte*' with verve and some scandalous *fioriture*. Nobody paid the faintest attention: now at home, thought Van der Valk, some piss-vinegar commissaire would have popped his nose out straight off to complain about levity.

Divisional commissaire Wollek was like an old grey wolf, his face, his voice, all his movements were as quiet as Chinese writing, done on silk with a sable brush, and Van der Valk liked him at once. He had the manners of a cardinal and thin delicate hands, and should have been sitting at a gilt-cornered table covered in Spanish leather, with the walls covered in Rubens paintings, but such things are not found in police bureaus.

'A cigarette?'

'Thanks.'

'Difficult for you, all this. But perhaps you could tell me your story.'

Van der Valk told, leaving out nothing.

'Yes. A king in a rainy country. One wonders what he was doing there – he would have found Paris more congenial.'

'The old gentleman, his father, is an old tyrant as I hear. He might have been very dictatorial.'

'The role of the wife is obscure.'

'It's all obscure. Luckily we're not called on to understand it. Nothing now but to notify all concerned and say we're sorry. I was one jump behind the whole way. I simply never had the facts to go on that might have helped me understand. They sent me off on this goose-chase, exactly as though they feared or suspected something serious would happen, yet the things they must have known – or feared – they never told me. Now I have to go back and tell them I've found him, and he's dead, under circumstances that almost look as though he had killed himself for fear I would find him.'

'I don't understand why they were in such a hurry,' suggested Wollek. 'The reason given was that he was an irresponsible person, as I understand, and might throw money about. Apparently he did throw money about. But with the amount of money involved, that is only a drop. He couldn't have remained hidden for very long, after all. Why the hurry? Why not signal him as a missing person and wait till he was noticed somewhere?'

'I've wondered the same thing. His wife behaved more as though she didn't want him found. It's possible that when the old man got to hear, he issued a dictatorial order that sonny-boy was to be traced and brought back to reason pretty damn quick.'

'I think we'll have to find out,' slowly. 'A French subject has died under obscure circumstances, on French soil. That means that I am responsible for any inquiry that may be made later. I'd better ring up Paris. This old gentleman sounds the type that might draw a lot of water. And perhaps you'd better notify the Germans, since you know these people in Köln. And of course his wife. Both these people will have to be formally identified. Would you like to use my telephone?' He pushed it across the desk towards Van der Valk.

'Yes.'

He rang Amsterdam. The Portuguese majordomo was full of regret, but he had not seen Anne-Marie, nor had he heard from her. It was peculiar, but since leaving Innsbruck, she seemed to have vanished. He rang Canisius. A private secretary, as full of silky regrets as any majordomo, told him that Mr Canisius was unfortunately away from home: they would be in communication with him that day – was there any message?

'No. Ask him to leave a number where I can reach him. It's extremely urgent.' They would do that. Would Mr Van der Valk be kind enough to ring again at five-thirty? That was extremely good of him.

'Polizei Praesidium, Köln. Herr Stössel, please . . . Heinz? Van der Valk. I'm in Strasbourg. End of the trail, I'm afraid. They're both dead. Double suicide. You'll have to get hold of the father and bring him over here. Office of Commissaire Wollek in Strasbourg. Yes, today – the sooner we get that over the better.'

'I'll arrange that,' came Stössel's distant, unemotional voice. 'In fact you've given me a job I'll have to do twice over. Your Mrs Marschal is here. Peculiar thing. She turned up here this morning. Said she wanted to see the girl's parents. She had a tale about persuading the girl to come back home directly she was found, and

107

so forth. I told her I was waiting to hear something from you. Wouldn't do to be precipitate.'

'How did she strike you?'

'Rather shrill and emotional. It would have made matters worse. She's staying here at Park – she said she'd stay here till I heard from you.'

'Sorry, Heinz. You'd better bring her along as well. She'll have to identify her husband, and make the usual arrangements with the authorities here – funeral and so on.'

'I'm just looking at the map. Frankfurt – mm – Karlsruhe . . . Looks as though it'll take about four hours on the road. You'd better expect me around six.'

'Very well. I'll be here.'

Mr Wollek was nodding gently – every Strasbourgeois can follow German.

'We'd better have lunch,' he said. 'Perhaps you'd like to come back to me here this afternoon.'

'I don't feel much like lunch.'

'Quite, and that's just the time to have a good one. You know this town at all?' His voice was paternal. These young men, it seemed to say. Getting upset about a death and not eating properly. 'I'll give you the address of a good place. I'd join you, but I'm afraid this has given me some extra work. Ask them for liver – it's still in season.'

*

The old boy was perfectly right; what was the use of getting in an uproar? There was nothing left but the details of administration. The French would do that. And Heinz Stössel, by a strange coincidence, had the job to do that nobody liked – breaking the news. He himself had nothing to do at all. The lieutenant of gendarmerie in Saverne was filling in forms, Mr Wollek in Strasbourg was there to make sure nothing went wrong, Heinz had a tedious and disagreeable drive in front of him from Köln – and he could twiddle his thumbs. He just didn't know why he felt so damned uneasy. He would go and have a proper meal and plenty to drink; it was a sour thought that he would put it on his expense sheet, which would go back to the police accounts in Amsterdam, and get sent on, eventually, to Canisius. The executors, as near as made no matter, of Jean-Claude Marschal, deceased. There was no point in thinking about that, either.

There was fresh goose-liver. Very simple, cut in slices and cooked in butter like any other kind of liver. Reinette apples went with it, sliced too and cooked soft in a spoonful of white wine. Van der Valk read the paper, drank a bottle of champagne, and was shamefacedly surprised to find that it had done him a lot of good. Arlette would have agreed. What would be the point, she would have asked with the same common sense as Monsieur Wollek, of sitting being miserable with a dried-out ham sandwich just because you are upset about a suicide? That makes no sense.

*

'You had a good lunch?' asked Wollek politely. He was sitting where Van der Valk had left him, in the same position. He had had his ashtray emptied, and the window opened to air the room.

'Very good. Did me no harm. I'm more tired than I had realized.'

'I can understand that. You were a little bit out of your depth, weren't you? Millionaires are not quite the same as other people, are they? Awkward kind of predicament. You were given ridiculous instructions, too. Nothing clear-cut, nothing defined. No crime, one can't quite see what all the fuss is about, why there is such a panic – the fact is nobody quite knew what they wanted. I've known similar things done. Then if anything goes wrong they can blame it handily on the investigating officer. He didn't understand his instructions, they'd say. Quite right too – omitting only the fact that there never were any proper instructions.'

Van der Valk allowed himself to grin for the first time in days, it seemed.

'Well, I can add a bit to this picture. I rang a colleague of mine in Paris, who has considerable experience of this financial set. Ask him which Rothschild is which and he'll tell you the whole family history and draw you a pedigree.'

Sounds like Kan, thought Van der Valk. They had one in Amsterdam like that too.

'I asked him about this Marschal. He knew about him all right. Said he was a bright and able fellow, but completely on the periphery of affairs. Quite frankly, his death wouldn't make a ha'porth of effective odds, to the structure of this business, or to the conduct of their affairs, or anything else. I asked whether the death could possibly create any reverberations, being a suicide, but he seems to think it would make none whatever.'

'But what about the old man?' asked Van der Valk. 'This is his son, after all. Heir, what's more, to a terrific fortune. The old man had made over a tremendous amount of money already to him, to avoid inheritance tax or whatnot. Nobody apparently knows quite how much. It's salted away in God knows how many different banks. This one had pretty big balances just on current accounts, under disguised names. I stumbled on that in Germany – they're all names of Napoleon's marshals!'

Wollek lifted an amused eyebrow.

'We'll find a few in Strasbourg then, maybe. Great breeding-ground for marshals. Romantic-minded chap.'

'What happens to all this vast quantity of Napoleonic poppy? Sounds like the buried treasure of the SS.'

'Yes, that's exactly what I asked. Our man in Paris doesn't know, but he says he can probably find out. He thought probably it all reverted to the old man, since the son died while he was still alive. The old man can presumably settle it on anything or anyone he pleases – if there are no descendants he can give it to the cats' home.'

'There are two children – both girls. He could perhaps make a trust fund or something.'

'He's going to find out. You see we have a right to ask, since this is, after all, a suicide. He knows this fellow Canisius who approached you, but only vaguely, since he doesn't run the French side of the business. There are two or three more of the same sort that sit in the Paris offices under the old man's eye. He'll probably ring me up this evening with whatever news he's managed to pick up.'

'I've got to ring this Canisius again anyway,' said Van der Valk, 'I'll see whether he can shed any light. I imagine the death will complicate things in some way, because it must be the reason they were so anxious to have Marschal traced in a hurry. Might have some bearing on the administration of the business. My boss back in Amsterdam must have been given a pretty strong reason to send me off after the man the way he did. Naturally he didn't tell me – I'm only a bum inspector of police. Mine not to reason why.'

Wollek smiled slowly.

'Prefects enjoy sending the police on that kind of damfool errand – with a few hints that the Ministry of the Interior will notice how smartly action is taken.'

Van der Valk made a sour face.

'I've always been good and sure there was more to all this than anyone saw fit to tell me,' with disgust. 'I suppose I might as well make this phone call – they'll be here from Germany in another hour. Can I use your phone again?'

The secretary in Amsterdam was abominably suave.

'Ah, Mr Van der Valk. Thank you so much for ringing. We have been in touch with Mr Canisius since you called. Unfortunately – most unfortunately – he is tied at present to some quite pressing business commitments. He asks me to convey to you his gratitude, and to assure you again – of course he realizes that it is quite unnecessary – of his confidence in your discretion and ability. He will be back in Amsterdam on Monday. Perhaps you could be so good as to make personal contact with him then.'

Van der Valk was irritated by all this creaminess.

'Where is he, exactly? This is a situation that needs his immediate attention.'

'Oh he realizes that: please reassure yourself. He particularly impressed upon me to be sure to make it clear that he quite understood how things stood, shall I say?' The suavity now had an unpleasant knowingness about it. Van der Valk took the receiver away from his ear and shook it angrily.

'Where is he? – just tell me that. Is he is Paris?'

'Mr Canisius has business in Spain,' said the secretary very

111

primly. Van der Valk felt veins in his forehead swelling. He forgot to speak French, and lapsed into an earthy Amsterdam Dutch.

'Look, Mr Buy-and-Sell, you tell me where I can get hold of Canisius if I need him or I can promise you faithfully that next week you'll be signing on at the Labour Exchange. Police business – you hear?'

'Mr Canisius generally stays on these occasions at the Prince de Galles in Biarritz,' very stiff now, and filled with distaste for badly-brought-up policemen. Mr Wollek, arms folded, had a faint smile.

'Pen-pusher,' said Van der Valk, putting the receiver back. 'By God I'd rather pick up empty ice-cream cartons with a pointed stick.' He made a small face of apology towards the Frenchman. 'One has to shout at them, you know – like in Germany.'

'We've got too polite,' gently. 'People take us for the man from the Inland Revenue. Sometimes I have to put this on my door.' He picked up a little plastic plaque that lay on his desk, with black letters engraved on it. '*Cave canem.*'

Van der Valk took it in his hand and laughed. It said simply '*Chien Méchant*'.

The telephone rang on the desk.

'Yes?... Send them up.' Wollek wiped the amusement off his face. 'Germany,' he said quietly.

Heinz Stössel spoke slow, quite good French with a clawky accent that did not make his pale impassive face any the less formidable.

'This is Commissaire Wollek of the Strasbourg police,' said Van der Valk formally.

'My sincerely-felt sympathies,' said Mr Wollek to Herr Schwiewelbein with equal formality, in the sing-song German of Alsace.

Mr Schwiewelbein was a man of fifty. His hair was brown and white in patches, both discoloured, his clothes and hat were clerical and neutral, and he had a carefully neutral face, but there was even now a military look about him. The outward signs were shoulders that he had never let stoop nor become rounded, and the heavy scar of a machine-gun bullet that had ploughed up one side of his

112

jaw and mutilated his ear, which had healed roughly and never been prettified. It showed too, less obviously, in a face that Van der Valk found strangely striking. There was a great deal of fortitude in that face, not that of a quick or particularly intelligent man, but like the centurion in the Bible, a man that could both take orders and give them, a man that could endure under fire, a man that would never lose a certain patient sweetness no matter how he was battered. He had sat down without any fuss on the nearest chair, his hat on his knees, waiting for three senior police officers from three different countries to find time to smash his world up for him.

They were waiting for Anne-Marie. She was in street clothes, a suit that Van der Valk could see had cost a great deal without quite knowing why he was sure. She noticed him studying it.

'Nina Ricci,' she said, with a touch of familiar sarcasm. She sat down in her chair again (she had got up to hang her coat next to Mr Wollek's sober dark-blue loden), put her hands in her lap, got a violent fit of shivering, controlled herself abruptly, and stayed quite still. There were no chairs for Van der Valk or Heinz Stössel, but neither of them cared.

'I am very pleased,' began Wollek gently in his funny German, 'to have the help of Herr Stössel and Mr Van der Valk, who both know much more about these circumstances than I do. You will understand, Madame und Herr, that these formalities are demanded by the law and I am here to fulfil them. The facts are very simple. Mr Marschal was staying in a house he owned not far from here in the company of a young woman, and for reasons we do not know put an end to both their lives. They were found by Mr Van der Valk, who was looking for Mr Marschal on behalf of his family as I understand, and he reported the facts to the local authorities. Both bodies have been brought to the city, and both will have to be formally identified, which is why your presence here was necessary. It is now quite late but it is good, as I judge, to get that done with. I don't doubt then but that the Procureur will give the authorization to make whatever arrangements you wish, tomorrow morning. I have seen to the necessary paper work. Shall we go?'

There was a black ID Citroën in the cobbled courtyard with a police driver. Mr Wollek signed to Anne-Marie and to Van der Valk, and got in himself. The two Germans got into Stössel's black Mercedes.

'Medico-Legal Institute,' said Wollek.

It would have been like a vile rehearsal for a funeral cortège but that the police driver, with the streets of Strasbourg emptying and darkening, wasted no time. Stössel, to keep up, had to make the tyres of the Mercedes squeal at the corners.

The nasty part was conducted in an equally brisk way. The attendant had a slight brassy smell of white wine about him, but dropped no stitches under Mr Wollek's eye.

'Will you formally identify the two persons found by you at the address named here?' in the precise metallic French of the Republic's judicial forms.

'I recognize them both and I do so formally identify,' said Van der Valk.

'Can you, Madame, identify this man as Jean-Claude Marschal and as your husband?'

'I do identify him – as both,' Anne-Marie's voice was as metallic as Wollek's, and much louder. It grated in the stillness.

'And can you, sir, identify the young woman as Fräulein Dagmar Schwiewelbein?'

'It is my daughter,' said the man simply, very quietly.

'May I have your signatures, please?'

*

They were back in the office. Wollek brought several papers together on his desk, turned them on end, and tapped them to get the edges level.

'Copies of these documents that you will need for your administration, Herr Stössel, will be made when we have the Procureur's signature of release. That should be done tomorrow morning. You know how clerks are – they go home at night.' Heinz Stössel, who had not said a word since coming, nodded with a very faint smile.

114

'One more formality. Herr Schwiewelbein, the scene of this tragedy has been carefully examined by the lieutenant of gendarmerie and has been inspected by the Substitute for the Parquet as French law requires. Some tests have been made by technicians under my control. Both observation by skilled officers and the laboratory tests confirm the appearances. Your daughter did not kill herself. She was shot and died instantly and painlessly at a moment when she was happy and peaceful. She may have been asleep. Immediately after, as far as can be judged, the man with her ended his own life.' Wollek paused for a fraction, flicked his eyes at Anne-Marie, and went on smoothly.

'This kind of suicide is in our experience not altogether an act of despair. I would myself, speaking as a man as well as a police officer, call it an act of love. Even an act of hope. I hope in my turn that this will lighten, if only a very little, your sorrow.'

That is a very clever man, thought Van der Valk. He too was looking at Anne-Marie, but she gave no sign, made no movement, said nothing.

'Thank you,' said the German. There was the same dignity in his voice as in his face. He hesitated for a short second and then went on.

'If I understood rightly, Herr Wollek, they were in bed together when they were found?'

Nod.

'They were making love then – when he shot her?'

'Yes,' said Wollek with no hesitation.

'You think he loved her?' Wollek glanced up at Van der Valk.

'There's no doubt of that.'

'I don't think there's any doubt either that she loved him,' said the German with an odd tranquillity. 'I can feel, at the least, that it was not altogether a waste.'

Anne-Marie still did not budge. She had taken a cigarette out of her bag: Heinz Stössel lit it for her.

'I was struck by your kindness, Herr Wollek. It confirms everything I had heard from Herr Stössel, who I had feared for a while was inventing a romance to try and relieve my pain and – what was very natural – to relieve his own painful embarrassment. You see, we spent four hours together in his car, coming here upon an errand of despair. Herr Stössel spent much of that time explaining to me that he was certain my daughter had been happy.'

Nobody could stop himself looking at Stössel, who did not move a muscle. Looking at that pale ham of a face, one would have said that the summit of feeling for the man would be a double helping of pork chop and fried potatoes with pickled cucumber. Van der Valk, who knew that Heinz had a child who was slightly mongoloid, rubbed his nose with a good deal more embarrassment than Stössel was showing.

'She had a week's happiness,' muttered the man – and he had looked like the kind whose highest pitch of emotion comes in finding that the quarterly accounts balance. 'A wonderful holiday in the mountains, all kinds of clothes, the pleasure of ski-ing that she loved, a shower of generous pleasures and presents – expensive autos . . . even the dodging about and running away must have seemed to her like a very exciting adventure. A romantic slice of life – and a romantic death. What more could a girl of that age desire?'

None of them said anything. Wollek picked up his sheaf of papers and slid them gently into a manila envelope, busying himself unnecessarily with fastening it. Herr Schwiewelbein got up.

'I will remember – my wife and myself – the consideration shown me by the police of three countries.' He walked out of the room slowly.

'I'll see to all that,' said Stössel. He punched Van der Valk lightly on the arm. 'Bad luck, that.' He shook hands gravely with Mr Wollek. 'Perhaps I see you tomorrow, Herr Kommissar. The formalities of bringing her home, you know.'

'Just come to me. Can I be of any service? – hotel or anything?'

'I fix all that.'

'Goodnight to you.'

It was indeed a romantic death, Van der Valk was thinking; it is a very good thing to find beauty in that. A piece of German lyric poetry. There is just one thing: it was just a scrap too well timed. The stove was still warm when I got there, and the two of them had not been dead four hours. When I got to Strasbourg, Jean-Claude and his tanzmariechen were still alive.

*

He turned his attention back to Anne-Marie. Death levelled everybody – the millionaire's wife, the sophisticated hostess of Amsterdam, had vanished; so had the gay siren of Innsbruck, the unaccountable downhill girl full of contradictions. One reached bedrock on these occasions: what sort of rock was at the base of Anne-Marie?

Wollek had changed his manner. A man who has lost his only daughter . . . but this was business.

'You have heard what I said, Madame. On a purely material plane, there is no reason for me to doubt the conclusions reached. Mr Marschal shot the girl, and himself. The Substitute is satisfied, and so am I. We have further the experienced observation of Mr Van der Valk. You have of course the right to query my findings, to see the doctor's report, anything you wish. Do you wish to make any statement or pose any question, before these papers go, as they will first thing tomorrow, to the Procureur for his signature?'

'No,' she said briefly. 'I would like to see the house. I would like Mr Van der Valk to show it me.'

Mr Wollek considered this, not afraid to be seen thinking it over and taking his time answering.

'That is quite fair. The Procureur would have no objection, and I can allow that without reference to him. It is certainly good that Mr Van der Valk accompanies you, since he knows a lot more about the attendant circumstances than I do. The house is of course under the jurisdiction of the Procureur. Yes. I will give the gendarmerie a ring, out there.'

'I have my car,' she said indifferently.

'Then I'll be with you in a moment or two,' said Van der Valk.

'You wish to conspire together,' she said with a sneer, putting on the coat he was holding for her. 'Afraid I'll kill myself as well? I'll be in that courtyard place: I want to stretch my legs anyhow.'

117

Mr Wollek looked at him with a half smile.

'Is it really technically all above board?' asked Van der Valk. 'That wasn't just for poor old Thingummy's benefit?'

'You find the death a little too pat, don't you?'

'Gunshot suicides are so easy to fake.'

'That's why we always check them ve-r-y carefully. That lieutenant wasn't happy either; that's why what you say doesn't surprise me.' The smile widened. 'I didn't have any lunch – neither did the doctor. The technical crew might have had a few drinks out in Saverne – but they did a thorough job. No hankypanky. I'm quite genuine – I can pass these papers to the Procureur tomorrow morning and he'll sign them, and that poor old chap can take his daughter home.'

'I'll take her out there, then. It's true enough – she has the right to see.'

'I'll phone them to give you the keys. By the way I found a message here when we got back from the Institute. Our man in Paris. He says that he's seen one of the managerial types of the Sopex. Your pal Canisius was there too, by the way. They didn't appear very perturbed about this death, just oh how tragic, etcetera. One point of interest – the old man appears to have gone a bit gaga. It's being kept very dark, for the good of the firm and so on, but apparently old Marschal is getting very old, and in consequence they let him say what he pleases, but they don't pay much heed. He trots into the office every morning still and upsets things, but they have a whole façade erected for him to play with, to give him the illusion that he's still completely in command. Whereas in reality the inner ring makes all the decisions.'

'There's certainly nothing left for me to do,' said Van der Valk with a laugh. 'I can trot back home tomorrow. I'll probably have the pleasure of her company, back to Amsterdam. She inherits all that fortune, I imagine. You could perhaps send me on an extract of the relevant papers when it's all signed – I can turn that in with a written report. Be glad to get back. We had an American soldier on leave knifed in the harbour quarter the day I left – kind of thing where all the witnesses are perjured.'

Wollek smiled sourly.

'I've had three hit-and-run auto accidents in three weeks. Depressing life, sometimes. Well, so long. If she seems to want to hang around here, let me know and I'll have an eye kept on her.'

'So long and very many thanks. Any time you're ever our way . . .'

'Only sorry I didn't get the chance to show you a bit of hospitality here. Well, I'm off home. My wife won't be too downmouthed – she's got a sister of hers staying with us. Quackquackquack, morning till night. Goodnight.' Van der Valk laughed, and ran quickly down the echoing staircase.

*

It was still that rented car, or if it wasn't it was one just like it; a faceless grey Opel like a hundred thousand more. Her skis were still strapped on the roof. She was sitting quietly smoking.

'You have to drive.'

'Huh?'

'I don't know the way.'

'Yes, of course.' The hired car was a better one than that he had had, but only because it was newer. It is a half-hour's drive to Saverne from Strasbourg and neither of them said a word the whole way, but he was conscious of her in a way so acutely sensitive as to be painful. She was sitting beside him in the small car in a loose, comfortable way, crowding in on him at corners; she had kicked off her high-heeled shoes and put on leather moccasins, and was sitting in a driving position, her knees apart and her skirt well above them. Her coat – it was the snobbish kind that has the mink on the inside instead of face to the world – was thrown open and instead of the disagreeable chemical smell that the insides of most German autos have there was a pleasurable scent of warm delightful woman. Every time they passed street-lamps – a light anything but kind – he had a glimpse of her profile. She had lost the hard, almost savage look she had kept throughout the time in Mr Wollek's office, and was looking young and vulnerable. He knew that just as in Innsbruck she was his for the taking

119

and not for the first time he felt defensive. There was a richness in the inconsistencies of the woman that he could not help admiring: whatever she was, she was not negligible.

Before Saverne they had to branch to the left and he had to drive slowly on the unfamiliar twisting road. There was nobody about, it was misty as well as cold and in the French countryside people are early abed. He stopped at the police post and a yawning gendarme gave him the keys as soon as he spoke his name: Mr Wollek had kept his word.

'You won't want me,' said the gendarme. It was warm and stuffy and there came a good smell from the apple he was eating. The house was only a hundred and odd metres further and all the houses around were dark and shuttered. There was no harm in leaving the auto on the street; to undo the gate and bring it in would only risk attracting curious eyes. He held the side door open for her and they went in.

It was miserable how the friendly little house had lost all warmth in that short space of time; it was icy cold, dishevelled by the police technicians, and already there was a coating of dust over everything. Anne-Marie looked about without curiosity.

'And you came here this morning? And found them dead?'

'Yes. Just too late. Everywhere I've been, it's been too late.'

'How could a fool like you hope to understand?'

'I'm very often a fool, and I've learned that sometimes situations make one look even more foolish than one is. It doesn't do to get upset on that account.'

'What a fool you are,' she repeated cuttingly. 'And how did you get to know he was here, you fool?'

'I guessed how he had got out of Austria. By following my nose I stumbled on the man that helped him. The man was an old acquaintance. Jean-Claude had been a bit too clever. Asked him to ring up if any fools like me came sniffing about.'

'Ring up? There's no phone here.'

'Quite so, but how do you know that?'

'Think you're clever or something? I see it. And I know it. Jean-Claude detested telephones. When he went to all the trouble of making this hideaway he would certainly have seen to it there was no phone.'

'The people in the village café have one, though.'

'You utter incompetent, ignorant imbecile. I told you to stop. I warned you that you were doing something you couldn't see the consequences of. Stupid lout. You went on blundering along and now you see the result. I offered you money. You could have had more money than you've ever earned in your life, all in one hand. I offered you myself. Do you think that I'm the kind of woman to sleep with the first hayseed oaf she meets at a wintersport station? No. You had to play honest stupid copper, too virtuous to live. You had to fi-nd him, because that's what you were to-old to do. There never was such a fool.'

Van der Valk sat down. On the dusty window-seat the stones on their socles glimmered: a little dust did not affect them. He looked a little like the knight in a set of chessmen. He picked it up: he hoped this was a good move for a knight.

'Your theory is that he killed himself because he knew I was after him, because he knew that he couldn't get away, because I would have barricades set up on all the main roads like after a bank holdup. So he killed himself just before I could get here?'

'No – fool – I don't believe that. He didn't kill himself. He was killed.'

'Really? Who by?' inquired Van der Valk politely. 'You?'

'Canisius, you blind imbecile. Canisius is sitting in Paris, finding it a fine joke.'

'You don't believe, then, in Mr Wollek's hypothesis of suicide?'

'I suppose I have to tell you,' she said in a suddenly dead, flat voice. 'There's no other way for it, now.'

'Please do. I need to have things spelt out. That's exactly what I've needed since this began. I'm tired of hints being dropped – I would like a few facts.'

'Canisius has been looking for years for a good opportunity to blackmail him.' Her hair had a dry, feverish look, but her voice was low and contained. 'It happened when we were only just married. Jean-Claude was much wilder then. He never thought that anything could possibly happen to him. He was the lucky one, he won everything – whatever stood between him and what he wanted just melted when he looked at it. We had been to the winter sports. Here in France, and Jean-Claude had a win. He was very gay and had had a lot to drink. He wasn't drunk, because he never was, but he was near it. We had a new sports car – you remember the first three-hundred SL – with the gullwing doors. Outside the town is a straight stretch of road, a sort of avenue; it's bordered by big plane trees. Jean-Claude got the idea of making the auto slalom in and out of those trees. I had a stopwatch from that day's competitions; we made bets about the time he could make. I suppose you can guess what happened. It was night and the place was deserted, but there was a man walking there with a dog. We never saw him till too late. He must have got frightened, thought we were chasing him or something round the trees. Anyway he lost his head and stepped out suddenly into the road. The auto only just touched him but it threw him against the tree. It was the tree killed him really.' She paused for a long sobbing breath.

'And what did the police do?'

'I don't know whether they did anything much. They must have taken it for pure accident. As I say it's a broad straight strip. Autos go fast along there, especially at night. The row of trees sets up a sort of chain reflection of the lights, and one couldn't see anybody who stepped out suddenly. I don't know even if they looked under the trees. It was dry, and there are tyre marks there anyway, because people park their autos under the trees in the daytime. But the man left a widow, you see. His name was in the paper. Jean-Claude was a very honest, impulsive person, and he got the idea fixed in his head that he would go to her, admit frankly that it had been him, say it was pure accident, ask her to understand and give her a lot of money to live on. Well I was horrified at that because I thought she would just blackmail him. I was very foolish myself, because I went to Canisius. He rushed straight to Jean-Claude of course, told him he mustn't do anything so foolish, and that he himself would pay the woman off without ever letting her know where the money came from or even that it was blood money at all.'

'I see. And why did the time come now several years later to use this piece of knowledge?'

'They've been fighting and plotting for years to get control of the business away from the Marschals. Well, they've succeeded. The old man is old, and has been getting potty. I don't believe he's really potty, but they're very clever at showing up eccentric things in the right light. They can get him declared incompetent by a court. But the money all belongs to Jean-Claude, and there's a huge amount. Even the old man didn't know how much there was. They want desperately to get their hands on all that. Yes, you can say, they control huge assets, and an enormous investment empire. But I happen to know they're not very liquid. They're hard up for ready cash, and this is how they planned to lay their hands on it.'

'Aha. Most interesting. So Canisius puts the screw on Jean-Claude, who loses his head and does a bunk. Canisius sends the police after him, thinking to harry him, make him lose his head, imagine that the police are actually after him on the old homicide charge. That's it, then?'

'But yes. Can't you see? That's why he ran away, in Innsbruck.'

'And that's why you called after him, in Innsbruck? To warn him?'

'Now you're beginning to understand.'

'You didn't know where he was yourself, so when you heard – from Canisius – that he was somewhere in Austria you thought that you'd tag along and by sticking to me find out where he was. When you saw that I was determined to get hold of him to find out myself what it was all about you tried to seduce me. When that didn't work all you could do was stay with me until I did find him and then hope to be able to warn him before I could talk to him. Huh?'

'Yes, that's right.'

'You know what I think?'

'Is that very important?'

'Not to him any more. To me it is. And to you maybe. I think you're a liar. Even a pretty bad liar, though quite a good actress.'

She glared. She opened her mouth and made a sort of spitting sound, then she thought better of it: she closed it again firmly, and controlled herself into complete stillness.

'Perhaps you're quite a fair liar in the sense that there's quite an adroit mixture of fact and fiction in this ridiculous tale you've been telling me so convincingly. I think it's true that old Marschal is gaga. Mr Wollek found that out this afternoon. I think it's true that Canisius and his pals would like to get hold of the money. About that liquidity story I wouldn't know and I doubt if you would either. I think it simply burns them to know that a huge sum of money is there and they can't get at it. I thought in the beginning of all this that Jean-Claude was simply a weak unstable kind of person with a flawed character, who ran away because he couldn't stand up to Canisius. Finding out, maybe, that his father was no longer in effective control of that gang of sharks might have pushed him into running away. But I'm no longer convinced of that line of reasoning. I think money just didn't have any proper hold on him. I think that he just got sick of the squalid squabble. That he's been sick of it for years, but that he stuck to his life there in Amsterdam out of loyalty to you and a sort of loyalty to his name. I think maybe that when you found out about your father-in-law you put a lot of pressure on your husband. To fight, to take his proper place, to get back control of the business, to be worthy of his father, to be worthy of you, and so on; I think that just disgusted him. He's always wanted to be free of the whole thing. He had bought this house several years ago. Every so often, when he could get away, after a trip and a business deal and some entertaining of important overseas customers and suppliers and so on, he came here, and pretended he was someone else for a few days. No more money talk, no more political manoeuvring, no more crap about the western alliance and doing business with the Russians or the Cubans or whatever. How he felt towards you I don't know. I find you a very attractive woman. Perhaps you're

124

a bit too intense, a bit too emotional, a bit too Spanish. You're anyway damn complicated. I don't know you well enough, myself.

'I think that he came to Köln, perhaps out of sheer coincidence, though he seems to have been reminded that there was a carnival going on. I think he saw and fell into conversation with a young girl, herself with very simple, honest, unsophisticated standards, and suddenly decided that this was what he wanted. I don't know what kind of wild idea he had. He must certainly have realized that she would be hunted for, and eventually traced. I imagine that he just didn't think because he didn't want to think. He was sick of planning and weighing consequences. He wanted to be free. His money could give him illusions of freedom, and this girl would supply him with more. He had seen every pleasure there was in life, and found them all pretty thin. He was like the king of the rainy country.'

'The what?' Anne-Marie had not understood: how should she?

Van der Valk picked up the volume of Baudelaire poems he had found, and that was still lying on the table – Mr Wollek's criminal brigade hadn't seen anything particularly incriminating in a volume of Baudelaire.

'Sure. Here. A poem. He read it, he knew it, he liked Baudelaire: they had a lot in common. Great gifts, great sensitivity, and a kind of tormented conscience. Baudelaire was always moaning about his bad luck, but he liked it really. He enjoyed his bad conscience and the feeling he was a doomed and tormented person. Jean-Claude understood that and sympathized with it. Here – read the poem. The hounds and the falcons – that's the sports cars and the skis and all the other things he did so well. The ladies-in-waiting with their lewd costumes – that's you, my dear, I rather think, striking sexy poses naked around that wonderful bathroom of yours. The subjects come to die under his balcony, the alchemist making the corrupt gold – he saw parallels there all right. And the green water of Lethe instead of blood. I think really that's why he ran off with his tanzmariechen. He wanted to prove that he still had blood inside him.'

She was no longer giving him the deer-eyed look. The eyes had narrowed and were watching attentively: she was missing nothing.

'I don't believe a word of all that tale of slaloms and SLs and plane trees. It has a slick fabricated sound. I think you've just made it up to convince me that Canisius is the sinister villain in this piece. You'd even like probably to convince yourself that it is so, and that he has caused your husband's death. Because I'm pretty sure that was provoked by nobody but you.'

He pulled himself up abruptly; he had said too much, and wanted to kick himself. He had just broken one of the cardinal rules of police procedure, which is to avoid any personal involvement in anything or anybody one comes across professionally. Stung by his own clumsiness and stupidity, he was now trying to demonstrate that he was really a clever fellow after all, he told himself sadly. The knight's move was wrong; there was too much of a bold sortie into unknown country about it. Anyway, this wasn't a game for knights; he should have moved a pawn, very cautiously and gradually.

She still wasn't saying anything, but she was looking at him with an oddly bright expectant look, her lips slightly parted. He picked up another of the stones, surprised at its weight. The cold smoothness was consoling to his moist hot hand.

It was not even as though there were any point in it. Even if he were certain that she had known about this house and had been in it, he could not prove it, and whatever she had done, it was nothing criminal – any more than Jean-Claude had done anything criminal. Both were victims of a peculiar fatality that they shared, that belonged to both of them.

'My husband is dead,' she said suddenly with something like hatred in the cold quiet voice, 'and you sit there, doubtless very pleased with yourself, telling me that I caused his death. To try and hide your own stupidity and ignorance from yourself. You understand nothing. There is the same miserable meanness and narrowness in your thinking as all the others show.' Others? What others, he wondered.

'When I saw you first in Amsterdam I thought that there might be some intelligence in you, that you had some scrap of sensitivity and understanding. Now I see that you are just like any other

126

policeman. Dutch, dim, obstinate, with your mean literal little mind. Get out of my sight. Find your own way back to Strasbourg. I don't have to listen to a fool like you trying to justify himself.'

He sat quiet and looked at her smilingly. Froth, my dear, by all means, if it makes you feel better, he thought. She stood looking at him a moment with contempt, then turned abruptly and left the room, shutting the door with a bang. He listened to her climb the stairs; over his head she stood still a moment in the room of the two pistol shots. He was sorry for her, but there was nothing he could do; there was nothing he could do at all, but get a carefully written report plotted out in his head. He would be asked for all the details, in Amsterdam. It would hardly be read, but that was unimportant: all that mattered really was to get it accepted. Heinz Stössel, in Köln, had a far more important and exacting piece of work. Since the sad thing was that nobody really cared about the Marschals; it was the little German shopgirl who had happily put on the carnival costume in which she looked so fine that would, rightly, be mourned. Marschal had had nothing left to do in this world: it was why he had shot himself, surely? He had realized that, perhaps, dimly. She had wanted to go with him, she had offered, she had even insisted: Marschal had yielded to that. It had been something to him, that she, at least, had not wished to leave him.

As for Anne-Marie . . . He could hear her now coming down the stairs, in the room next door, looking round, taking leave of the pathetic remnant of Jean-Claude's deceptions. Then he heard the other door slam, and the click of the gate on to the street. Well well. There wasn't much he could do about that!

The speculations were quite fruitless, after all; exactly how the links had been laid that made up the chain of reactions culminating in this death was not important now. He himself was among those links, in actions he had made or provoked. He hadn't understood, but there was little enough point in tormenting himself with that. He should have understood, in Innsbruck, but the glitter of the snow on the mountains, the intoxication of the air, the speed and beauty of the girls ski-ing – everything had bemused him, confused his thoughts and stupefied his mind.

I am just a plodding Dutch plainsman, he told himself; I was quite straightforwardly out of my depth. He felt the contour of the stone in his hand with his mouth and tongue, as though he were blind and was trying to reach something with other senses, that he used clumsily through lack of practice. The stone was just a stone; none of its beauty and richness could be reached that way. He put it down with a sigh and reached in his inside pocket for his note-book and a ballpoint.

Canisius had been manoeuvring to get the last of the Marschals into a position of impotence. That was not difficult, but to find a way to lay hands on all that money was more difficult. When Marschal had bolted he had seen an opening at once. Marschal was an irresponsible, wild, reckless character, and might do or be led to do something unbalanced, and that might give him a valuable handle. Naturally, Canisius had been delighted to hear that Marschal had run off with a teenage girl in Germany; nothing could have suited him better. And to confuse the situation still further, he had maliciously told Anne-Marie – her high-voltage emotions injected into the situation would doubtless tangle things still further. Astute.

Jean-Claude was not really the last of the Marschals. Anne-Marie was an obstacle as well. One would never find out how much she knew or guessed, or what Canisius suspected she might know or guess, but the man, who she had said once, contemptuously, had the mind of a grocer, and yet a clear insight into her character. Canisius had seen the contradictions of her nature.

Her '*espagnolisme*' – the 'Spanishness' that was one of her salient features, for instance. She would be maddened by Jean-Claude's stupidity and heedlessness in picking up the tanz-mariechen, and she would also be crudely and furiously jealous of this meaningless chit that meant somehow more to her husband than she had herself.

She had followed the turns of Canisius' mind without being able to realize that she was herself hopelessly enmeshed.

She might not ever have realized that in coming to this house – she had certainly come, Van der Valk was quite convinced of that –

she would precipitate a climax. And he himself had pointed it out to her. He shook his head; she had been quite right: stupid, blind, mean and narrow of mind and sight . . . there was a kind of fatality in that too. He should have kept more of an eye upon her, instead of running so frenziedly off to Chamonix. He was involved in these people; from the moment Canisius had stepped so delicately in his fur coat and beautifully-polished shoes into the office in Amsterdam he had been bound to them and he had never got any proper detachment, had never extricated himself. He had been half-seduced by Anne-Marie without realizing it, and had never managed the grip on the situation he must have to keep in control of it. He had been in a sort of trance, seduced and hypnotized.

He had better get out of this. That house was adding to his persistent sense of impotence. He put the stone – he still had it in his palm – back on the wide windowsill, snapped the light out and shut the door behind him. He supposed that Anne-Marie would inherit all Jean-Claude Marschal's worldly goods, but that huge quantity of money settled on him by his father . . . the old man was still alive. Could one revoke that kind of bequest? Canisius, doubtless, could have the best of legal advice on the question.

There was something wrong about the hall. It struck him at once, but it took some minutes to find what was changed or missing. Then he noticed; as usual, it was the kind of thing that is so obvious one cannot understand why one had not seen it instantly.

The rifle that had been hanging above that deer-antler hatstand affair – a French monstrosity with a shield-shaped looking-glass in the middle of it, and little hooks for one's clothesbrush and shoehorn – was no longer there. Was it possible that the gendarmerie had taken that away?

*

Even then he had still been in his trance. With a kind of stiff slowness he had gone back to the bureau of the gendarmerie to return the keys; they had rung a taxi for him to take him back to Strasbourg. By the time he was there he felt ready to believe he was making a fool of himself. Wollek's technical squad, finding a firearm death, had taken the rifle for examination. He knew of course that this was ridiculous; anybody with the scrappiest training in firearms could see that both deaths had been caused by the pistol found on the bed. Why should Anne-Marie have taken it, though? What on earth would she do with such a thing? It certainly was not to commit suicide. First, suicide was not in her nature; second, women do not take a hunting rifle to kill themselves with: they would not know how to handle so awkward a weapon.

He had better warn them that Anne-Marie was loose somewhere with a hunting rifle – rather a naughty weapon too; he had not looked closely at it, but it had been a heavier calibre than an ordinary twenty-two. One didn't even know whether there was any ammunition for it; surely Marschal had not been fool enough to leave the thing hanging up there loaded?

He would get no thanks from the French police. If he told them that he was certain Anne-Marie had been in that house before, had even provoked the double death, they would look at him in a stony way, silent: he had no evidence of any such thing. If he made a fuss, the only thing that could happen would be the sending of a call to all police to have Anne-Marie picked up, and in the meanwhile, the Procureur would refuse to sign the papers releasing the deaths from further inquiry. His signature meant that the judicial authorities were satisfied, that the body of the tanzmariechen could be taken home and buried and prayed over, that the press, scenting no further excitements, would leave Herr Schwiewelbein in peace.

He rang the unpretentious hotel where the two Germans were staying. Anne-Marie had not registered there. No, that was natural enough; she would choose the most palatial hotel in the town.

She had; she had also booked out again an hour ago, and had paid the forfeit without even looking at the bill. The porter had carried her expensive dressing-case. He had fetched her car round to the front for her – Yes, that was right, a grey Opel: quite unmistakable – there was a bundle of skis on the rack, in one of those sort of rainproof canvas sacks.

Van der Valk, who did not wish to identify himself as a policeman or anything like it, gave this porter a ten-franc note. Had she said or asked anything? Yes, she had asked for a main road towards the south-west; he had pointed her out the Schirmeck road.

Van der Valk went off to think this over with a road map. Schirmeck – St Dié – yes, it went over the Vosges in a south-westerly direction towards Epinal: now what could be the point of that?

She couldn't be heading for Chamonix, could she, having known that was where he had got his information from? And what would she do there anyway? And if she were, why take that road? If she were headed for the mountains she would surely take the logical way south through Colmar and Mulhouse and the Belfort gap. He let his finger waver along the network of roads heading vaguely south-west; his finger reached Dijon, hesitated, wavered on. Moulins . . . Montluçon, or Clermont-Ferrand – it made little odds; the roads ran on, either Brive or Limoges, but they both came out at the end at Bordeaux. What along all these routes with their possible turnings could interest Anne-Marie? She couldn't be heading for Paris: she would have taken the Nancy road. He made casts up and down, zigzagging with his finger like a dog on a scent. He was back at Bordeaux without a flicker of light illuminating his mind, and let his finger wander vaguely along the coast. La Rochelle? Down – he stopped suddenly. In the extreme south-western corner, tucked in the angle formed by the French and Spanish coasts, his finger was resting on Biarritz. It was suddenly clear to Van der Valk what Anne-Marie was doing with a hunting rifle slid in between the skis on her auto roof.

Of course he could get Wollek out of bed. The more he thought about this the less he liked it.

He had a rented car too, didn't he? And she had only an hour's start.

*

What was it Anne-Marie had called him? Slow and obstinate, mean and narrow, stupidly literal-minded, very Dutch. He sighed heavily and opened the window beside him to let the smoke out of the auto and get a bit of oxygen into his bloodstream. That was quite true. He couldn't help it either, he had been born that way, trained that way, and his daily life only settled him further into the grooves of official rigidity. He was a professional. It is only in books that one finds the brilliant amateur detective X; real policemen are obstinate and hardheaded, are slow and literal-minded, are frequently mean and nearly always narrow: they have to be. They are part of the administrative machine, a tool of government control, and in our days the government, in order to make head against the pressures and distortions, the tides of economic change and the winds of upheaval, must possess a machine so complex and so detailed that its tentacles can grip and manipulate every soul within its frontiers. That is a job for professional civil servants, not for amateurs. Holland, thought Van der Valk, with its inexhaustible supply of good administrative lance-corporals, possesses a wonderful machine, of which he was part. The trouble with Holland was indeed that the machine was far too good. It was so detailed, so perfected, so rigidly armoured against attack or pressure, that if it did break down it took a year to get it back on the rails. There is nobody that can improvise, nobody that can imagine, nobody capable of independent effort. All the wooden dollies, so perfectly co-ordinated, jerk about in agony mouthing and gesticulating, waiting for a super-professional that can pull the master string. Which is very hard to find. All the soldiers are lance-corporals, all the officers are colonels, they are all absolutely admirable, and there isn't any general.

People often said that England was the opposite, that it was a country run by amateurs on the old-boy network. Van der Valk did not know a great deal about it, but he rather doubted that. He had met some English civil servants, and seen how carefully trained and selected they were. Of course there was the parliament and the government, full of public-school types getting together in clubs exchanging passwords about prep and hols, but he thought that they were pretty unimportant: they talked a great deal, but they did very little. The English might remain convinced that their famous parliament was the seat of might and decision, but they must secretly know that countries nowadays were not run by talkative old Etonians that had been brilliant in the debating society and had got a third in history at Oxford.

But one needed amateurs too, as Holland showed. A country needed huge armies of thoroughly trained professional administrators, and surely it needed large numbers of poets and philosophers, eccentric persons who knew nothing about productivity statistics but all about Etruscan civilizations? It wasn't enough to fill your government with eager beavers that all had a first-class degree in economics.

Take this situation. What could a professional policeman do in these circumstances? His famous rules and procedures were all meaningless – nobody had broken any laws. A professional policeman, if he had any sense, would have washed his hands of it at once, turned his back resolutely. Mr Marschal's wanderlust, Mr Canisius' devious twitching at the thread, the tortuous whims of Anne-Marie and the over-simple, over-ingenuous impulses of little Dagmar – any sensible policeman would shake his head with a smile and return to the comfortable, professional, exactly posed-and-pegged-out problem of how to stop jewel thefts.

Of course the fatal mistake – going after Marschal at all – had been right at the start; the Chief Commissaire of Police, a professional and a bureaucrat to his fingertips, had fallen head-first, delightedly, into the pit directly Canisius had stepped with his beautiful shoes on the concealed button that released the trapdoor. Van der Valk had not been able to turn back; the typical Dutch mistake had been made of fiddling obsessively at the individual till he got back into line.

He felt sure that in England they would have been wiser. A Commissioner or a Superintendent or whatever it was they had there – the high pooha of the police – would have listened to Canisius with old Etonian courtesy, and murmured in a veiled way that under the circumstances he did not really see his way . . . there were, of course, or so he understood, er—private detectives (dirtiest of all dirty words) . . .

A private detective, the beautiful unspoiled darling of a

detective story, would of course have leaped straight into bed with Anne-Marie, given Canisius the old right hook straight to the shiny false teeth, beaten Marschal by two seconds flat on the Olympic Piste at Innsbruck, had the tanzmariechen fall in love with him instead, and been paid ten thousand pounds on the last page by grateful millionaires.

And here I am, thought Van der Valk ruefully. I've made every mistake I could have. I haven't been professional, I'm not clever enough, being much too Dutch, to be an amateur, and now, as a fitting climax to so much inefficacity, I'm driving across the whole breadth of France in a hired Renault when, obviously, I should be burning up the highway in James Bond's Aston Martin. What I need is a world like Kipling's India, where natives are natives, subalterns are sensitive and self-sacrificing, the whole world is ruled by the Widow of Windsor, and there isn't a single thing that a twenty-one-year-old journalist doesn't understand perfectly in the space of fifteen hundred words. Ichabod: a glory is departed.

Fair Ichabod O'Man – Mr Polly was one of Van der Valk's favourite characters. (Now if Mr Polly had tried that lark now-adays, the police would have had him in a second less than no time for Conveying Passengers without a Licence. What, in charge of a punt, and no diploma for punting?)

A Dutch policeman was really good for only one thing, and that was filling in a form explaining how some other very naughty asocial individual had filled in another form incorrectly.

His petrol tank was getting low and he had to keep a lookout for one of those large French notice-boards saying TOTAL 2 KM. That was it; nothing was really important any more. All poetry and all wisdom were in that simple phrase. Total two kilometres. Total knowledge, total safety, total destruction. Only two kilometres to go.

The alert reader will have noticed that he was very tired. Total two kay em. Everything else, to quote Mr Polly, was sheer sesquippledan verblejuice.

*

A sensible policeman – a professional policeman – would have stopped several times on the road for solid provincial French meals, a good night's sleep between sheets. Come to that, a professional policeman would never have embarked at all upon as ridiculous a goosechase as this one. He would have rung up Canisius. He would have rung up the gendarmerie of the Department of the Basses-Pyrénées and told them to stop a grey Opel Rekord with a bundle of skis on the roof. After all, from Strasbourg to Biarritz is just about one thousand kilometres by road. Twelve hours' driving; if you were very young and resilient, an excellent driver in a powerful auto, and you had had a good night's peaceful rest, and you started at dawn, and had good weather and fairly uncrowded roads, you could do it in a day with a two-hour break for lunch. You would need to be pretty good. Either a famous amateur in an Aston Martin – back again – or a professional seasoned on intercontinental rallies.

Van der Valk was doing it because there was no space here for a professional any more. He had no evidence that Anne-Marie even had the gun, he had no evidence that she was even going to Biarritz. Nobody in the world would have believed him if he shouted at the top of his voice that he knew, with absolute certainty, she was heading for a professional financier in a fur-collared overcoat and a Paisley silk scarf and a grey trilby hat – how would types like Canisius dress themselves in a place like Biarritz? – with the fixed idea of planting a bullet in him: it was too unlikely. Things like that do not happen, least of all in Biarritz, a pleasant town once favoured by His Majesty the King of England and Emperor of India, and now thought highly of by the new French upper class known as the 'cadres'.

The fact was that the cleavage between professionals and amateurs was here shown at its sharpest. Marschal – the old Marschal – had been a survivor of nineteenth-century banditry. A brilliant adventurer, like an American railroad king. Just the type Kipling would have recognized and appreciated – Harvey Cheyne. In our days, a sort of coelacanth. Everybody is convinced

135

it is extinct, and the rediscovery creates a fearful hullabaloo in scientific circles.

Canisius was the modern professional financier, at home in modern circles of power and influence. The presence of the old man, that glaring anachronism, had stuck in his throat for years. But senility and delusion helping, he had successfully set Monsieur Sylvestre Marschal aside. Remained the young Harvey Cheyne, Jean-Claude. He would have liked to tip him overboard into the Atlantic, but financiers don't do such things.

Anne-Marie, and not her husband, was the last of the Marschals. It was ironic; the old man had done all he could to improve his 'image', as the publicity boys had it: the formal, beautiful, sombre house in St Cloud was a peculiar setting for a man like that, whom one imagined more easily in a restless, vulgar atmosphere – the hotel room in Lisbon: wasn't that where 'Mister five per cent' – in many ways a similar figure – had lived and died? And he had wished to found a dynasty like the Rothschilds. That was a good example; they were as professional as you could wish, but they knew the value of the amateur mind. Old Marschal had succeeded in marrying his son off to a most suitable person, convent bred, the chateau-dweller, with a considerable fortune in land, an ancient name, and Parisian first-night looks. A little wild, but ski-ing was quite a respectable sport, and she would be tamed by chinchilla furs and diamonds.

But she had had a streak of buccaneer's blood that ran true to old Sylvestre's, and she had somewhere a confused feeling of loyalty to the Marschals. She had seen the direction behind the mortally slow and tortuous insinuations of Canisius and his tribe, she had seen the way the old man had been gradually trimmed by legal sidling, she had tried to whip up Jean-Claude and he had failed her. With his aristocratic instincts, his long nose in which money stank, his fine hands to which the stinking pennies would stick if he let them – a Marschal! Who could tell what efforts she had made, what pressure she had put on the man before he bolted? He had bolted, and had promptly caved in utterly.

And now Anne-Marie was on her way to strike a last blow for

136

the Marschals, with a rifle. God knew what she was thinking; quite possibly she imagined that that was what the old man would have done in similar circumstances.

She had known something about the little house in a Vosges village. The extraordinary performance Jean-Claude had put on at Innsbruck must have destroyed much of what balance she had left. For – Van der Valk saw that now clearly – the man had not run away from him, nor from the police in general, nor from Canisius: he had run away from his wife. And he had taken absurd melo-dramatic risks to make it clear to her. She had got the message; she had gone to the little house for one last plea, perhaps. Jealousy of the girl had complicated and confused her ideas further, and Jean-Claude had reacted in one way that she had not, perhaps, foreseen. Or was she familiar with the tale of Crown Prince Rudolf von Hapsburg?

What had the police of Wien done when they heard about the events of Mayerling? It was thought they had known, that they had been warned beforehand. They had been sensible: they had refused to know, refused to meddle. They had shown more sense than the Chief Commissaire of the Amsterdam Police, who had been impressed by the Sopexique, and had had a real Dutch mistrust of the house in the Keizersgracht and its inhabitants . . .

He was too tired. He had started at night, after a difficult day: he had had a good few thousand kilometres in his bones before beginning this absurd chase. For the sake of the shaky old man in Paris, for the sake of an innocent girl's parents, for the sake of Jean-Claude, who had made an effort for a scrap of peace and happiness, and yes, for the sake of Anne-Marie herself – he had liked her – he wasn't stirring up the whole French police apparatus. He was a fool and an amateur, but this had to be done in an amateurish way. He was going against a woman with a rifle – had she any idea how to use it? – with his bare hands like Bulldog Drummond. But he was too tired. If he went on this way there would be an accident, and he was too much of a policeman not to know that as tired as that he was a menace. It was dawn; traffic would be thickening on the roads. He could not get into Biarritz that evening. Van der Valk pulled the Renault into the side of the road somewhere not far from Moulins – he had the difficult mountain roads of the central massif of France ahead of him – and slept while the day came up like thunder behind him in the east.

*

When he woke he looked at his watch and made a face to see how late it was. But Anne-Marie would have to rest too, somewhere. She might even be near him. There was of course no guarantee she was on the same road and he had had no great hopes of seeing or catching the grey Opel. But she would not have reached Biarritz before the middle of the night any more than he would. And Canisius would be deep in pleasant dreams in a luxury suite facing the sea, on the second floor of the Prince de Galles.

He had breakfast at the first place he came to; nothing particularly wonderful looking, but the coffee was hot and strong. They cut him huge slices of ham, boiled three fresh eggs for him, took him for one of those crazy Englishmen that drive their autos the whole way to Spain on the wrong side of the road, and charged him a fortune. He didn't care – Marschal money. The only important thing was that Canisius should not know what efforts were being made on his behalf: he knew that this was really why he had chosen not to warn the French police about the rifle in among the skis. If Canisius heard – and he would hear – that she was gunning for him she was a dead duck: nothing else stood between Canisius and all the Napoleonic bank accounts strewn about Europe. As long as Anne-Marie was not a criminal she inherited, surely, the Marschal money, and she had two children, two girls. Van der Valk had thought about those two girls at their convent in Brussels often, the more since seeing the dead body of the tanzmariechen in bed in that room – her hair had been tousled and the wound hardly showed at the entry point: she had looked fourteen.

Did Anne-Marie know Biarritz well? Did she know where Canisius would be staying? What his movements were, what his

138

habits were? What sort of plan was she making, there somewhere ahead of him in the rented Opel?

*

He got in around one in the morning, and felt fairly safe. He had hoped originally to be there by ten the previous night but before he was past Dijon he had known this would be impossible. He parked the auto in a quiet spot, found to his relief that the early-morning temperature in Biarritz was some six degrees higher than it had been in the mountains, and tapped his forehead four times. He would be awake at four.

Coffee in the Station Buffet – it was like Innsbruck all over again, or Chamonix. This was a story of coffee in the early mornings in station buffets; Van der Valk, who had been a police-man for nearly twenty years, had known many more of those stories. He felt horribly middle-aged, but there were points in being professional. He had reached forty without getting shot, and that was more than James Bond had succeeded in doing!

Still, the station buffet was like a leitmotiv in Wagner – it meant, he rather thought, drama boiling up not far away.

He struck up a variety of casual acquaintances in the station, among others a Customs man, who told him about the Spanish frontier – the river Bidassoa! One didn't get away from the Marshals; if he had ever heard of the Bidassoa, it was because of Soult in Spain in 1813! He found the bookstall woman too, and though her stall was not yet open she had got some parcels to unpack, and some Paris papers off the night train to Irun, and she let him have a Michelin which he studied carefully. He did a good deal of driving around in the pale early sunlight, and decided that Biarritz was a nice place. Arlette would like it, here. Be a fine place for a holiday, though the prices, even out of season, would make her shudder. Still, they weren't – much – higher than in her precious Department of the Var.

He had a wash, a comfortable shave, drenched himself in eau-de-cologne, changed his slept-in suit, and felt almost human,

human enough to risk the early morning snootiness of the Prince de Galles's reception desk.

'I'm afraid that Mr Canisius is not yet awake.'

'When's he have his breakfast sent up?' The pale creature consulted the Spirit of Tact, balanced the results against the cherished principle of being as Rude as you Dare to Unknown Persons, and reached languidly for one of his telephones.

'Eight o'clock.'

'Five to now. Give him just a teeny buzz and tell him my name.'

With reluctance, this was done, in a hushed tone of noiseless respect.

'Mr Canisius asks you to be good enough to wait ten minutes. A page will take you.'

'Thank you, young man,' said Van der Valk in the tones of the Dowager Duchess.

A thin elegant floor-waiter – like all floor-waiters he looked a great deal more distinguished than the guests did – was wheeling out a trolley. There was a tinkle of silver and porcelain going on, a smell of hot chocolate – Madame de Sévigné – a whiff of after-shave – Yardley lavender – and overall that indefinable hotel smell of old carpets. Mr Canisius, cosseted and comfortable, was breaking bread on his little balcony, in a nervous-looking way, as though a paper snake on a spring might suddenly come whizzing out. Van der Valk, who had noticed that all foreigners in France do this, probably frightened of getting crumbs on the carpet, thought of Raymond Chandler, who described himself as being yes, extremely tough, even known to have broken a vienna roll with his bare hands.

Like all business men, Mr Canisius looked utterly indecent in pyjamas, though they were a restrained maroon colour, with edgings of thin silver cord, quite correct. He was also considerably too grand to stand up or shake hands with policemen at breakfast, but he nodded amicably, patted his lip with a fringed napkin, and said 'Quite a surprise. How are you?' in his soft milky voice.

'Tired.'

'Sit down. Have you had breakfast?' Van der Valk sat in a

rococo cane rocker with buttoned cushions and looked out at the expensive view across the Avenue de l'Impératrice to the lighthouse.

'Yes thanks.'

'But how did you know I was here?'

'Your secretary told me.' A slight frown disturbed the milky surface.

'However, don't be hard on him; I had to twist his arm.'

'Yes – there is some property of the company's in Spain, and this is quite an old haunt of mine. So I combine a little necessary supervision with a little fresh air and exercise. Golf, you know.'

'Ah yes. He mentioned that you had business in Spain, but no more.' Canisius nodded approval of this discretion.

'We have certain investments in housing along the coast. As you probably know, flats and bungalows there have had a spectacular success with the European public. I like to keep an eye on the building projects. In fact I will have to ask you to excuse me very shortly, since I have arranged with one or two of my associates to pay a little visit this morning.'

'Oh, it can wait till you get back,' said Van der Valk. 'Unless you happen to be late coming back.'

'By no means. It is about a hundred kilometres and we shall be lunching there, but I will be back at around three this afternoon. You wish to give me all the details?'

'Yes. It is a fairly complex business and I thought it right to come and see you personally, straight away.'

'Excellent, excellent. I am most appreciative, believe me, of the zeal you have showed throughout this unhappy business. Pity that you weren't in time to prevent that very sad death.' There was something about these words, mouthed by a business man in maroon pyjamas drinking cocoa, that irritated Van der Valk.

'The truth about the very sad death will not appear in the written report I will make to my superiors.'

'You're being rather enigmatic. I'm afraid that I know nothing but the bare fact of the death, and that I only learned in quite a roundabout way from the police in Paris.'

'Oh there's nothing at all doubtful about the death itself. That's perfectly plain sailing from the administrative angle. Indeed the authorities there in Strasbourg cut the formalities to a minimum in order to spare unnecessary pain to the girl's parents.'

'Ah, of course – I recall your telling me about this girl – a German girl?'

'Quite right. For similar reasons, I left a variety of things unsaid in my dealings with the police, and I will do the same in my own report at home. That is why I thought it better to have a conversation with you before going back to Amsterdam.'

'Now I begin to follow.' Mr Canisius had finished breakfast. He was in less of a hurry now to get rid of Van der Valk. He took a Super Maden from a square yellow box and lit it with an elegant waft of delicate Egyptian tobacco that went well with the hotel smell.

'I am very pleased,' he went on carefully, 'that you have shown the very qualities of discretion that were needed. If the press had chosen to make a drama of this affair it might have been most unfortunate.'

'I'm only a policeman, and I have not very much experience of millionaires. I've seen quite a bit of Mrs Marschal.'

'Very sensitive, highly-strung woman,' said Canisius gravely. 'You had to break the news to her, of course – a most disagreeable duty, I'm afraid. She took it badly?'

'She was quite calm. But she behaved oddly.'

'I see it all,' Canisius broke into a warm, friendly smile. 'She feels that her husband's death should be blamed on someone, isn't that it?' He had got up and was walking about with a kind of jerky animation. 'Quite possibly she has made meaning hints as to some malign influence I had upon her husband, who I'm afraid had rather a weak character. Something like that, hey?' He waved his cigarette at Van der Valk in quite a roguish way.

'Yes, various remarks have been made. Nothing substantial.'

'Well well, that's all quite easily explained. An explanation is certainly due you after all the pains you have taken, and one must certainly be given you. I shall have to let you into a few confidences.

However, unfortunately – most unfortunately – that will have to wait a little. Perhaps this evening. Yes, this evening, since you cannot be kept hanging round here, can you, though Biarritz is quite an agreeable spot, what? Now why don't you pass a quiet day here – all your expenses continue to fall to my charge, naturally, and may I suggest then that you come to dinner with me here tonight – would eight o'clock suit you? – and I'll straighten all this out, and then you can go back to Amsterdam and write your report, because I'll tell you quite frankly that your superior officer has no more information than you had yourself at the start of this. Dear dear, I had no reason to believe that it would have a tragic end, though of course I was alive to the possibility of something unbalanced. That was why I chose a responsible police officer, and not one of these private agents, persons with little sense of responsibility. Interested in nothing but the amount of money they can succeed in making for themselves. I'm delighted, simply delighted, at your acumen and tact. But yes, we'll discuss all that this evening, shall we?' He had gone milky again.

'Sure.' I hope we can both of us count on this evening appointment, thought Van der Valk.

'Now I'm afraid I must interrupt this, interesting though it is, since my car will be waiting for me in just half an hour. This evening then? Perhaps seven thirty, in the bar here? Splendid, splendid.'

Van der Valk, who hated lifts, walked down two broad flights of ambassadorial stairway contentedly. He wasn't sure that splendid was the right word. But Mr Canisius had talked too much. From viewing Van der Valk's sudden appearance in Biarritz with a lack of enthusiasm he had suddenly become that gentleman's very closest friend. Endearing of him.

*

He walked about the public rooms with nonchalance, staring a good deal out of the windows, amusedly aware that an underporter was keeping an eye on him just in case he was planning a raid on some old biddy's jewels. There was no sign of Anne-Marie, nor of

143

a grey Opel. Was he imagining the whole thing? Had he been strung up by fatigue and the dramatic performances of the Marschal family into imagining a romantic curtain to the third act? That was quite an easy conclusion to reach, but he did not think it was the right one. Tired as he was he had still two sides to his head, he hoped.

Jean-Claude Marschal was the northern type he had thought about that night and morning walking round Innsbruck, the theatrical type, who commits crimes, such as suicide, theft-of-a-government-helicopter, or abduction-of-a-minor-of-the-female-sex with a flourish and a bow to the audience. Anne-Marie was not like that at all; lying in wait for somebody with a gun was no stranger to her than it was to a Corsican farmer whose sister-in-law has an assignation with the farmer-over-the-hill's Lothario of a son. There was nothing, he had thought and still thought, intrinsically improbable about this at all, though it was not an idea that would occur to a Dutch policeman.

There was no need for her to hang about a hotel entrance waiting for Canisius to show himself. She almost certainly knew Biarritz well, and might also know all about Canisius' business there: presumably there was no secret about the little towers of beach apartments. (They were very big, but looked little, he thought, because they looked so flimsy – they were invariably the kind of architecture you get when you build a tower of matches laid across each other at right angles.) Quite the contrary, those things were a sure-fire moneyspinner for the Sopexique; they sold like ice-creams on a hot day at the zoo. It was possible that once knowing that Canisius was in Biarritz she would know perfectly well he would travel along the road leading to the border and Irun.

Knowledge like that made this one of the easiest kinds of assassination going, as everybody in the world knows since the day Mr Kennedy took a ride in an open auto through Dallas. Nor was there anything odd about a woman getting the idea. A rifle, one tends to think, is essentially a man's weapon, but any woman can learn to shoot, once she is not afraid of the gun. It is simply a question of the right position, uncramped and comfortable, and then looking along the sights: lying down, a woman can shoot as well as a man can. A highpowered rifle has a big kick-up from the recoil – but that is after the shot. At a range of say one hundred metres, and with a slow-moving target, one shot would be all that was needed, with a bullet that size. It would be similar enough to shooting with the old Lee-Enfield of Van der Valk's army days; at three hundred metres the rawest recruit learned in a day to bang down a target four foot square. Which meant a man at one hundred.

Anne-Marie, an ex ski-champion, was not going to be either scared of the bang or disconcerted at any technical difficulty – loading the thing, adjusting the sight, getting the safety off. He tried to remember whether the rifle had had a telescopic sight.

Canisius coming out of a hotel door would make an ideal target. But there was no square or anything with handy windows; opposite the Prince de Galles was nothing except the pompous boulevard and the still silky Atlantic: no perspective and no cover.

Somewhere along the road, where there were little hills, patches of greenery and shrubbery, clumps of trees . . . ? But the auto would be running at fifty kilometres an hour. Unless one was dead in line, the sights nearly parallel to the road, the shot was impossible: it would be like trying to shoot a partridge with a twenty-two. Where then would the auto slow down? At the frontier, obviously, to show the papers, but he had understood, from his acquaintance in the customs with whom he had gossiped at the station that morning, that the frontier was in Hendaye, where the National Ten ran straight out of the little town across the bridge over the Bidassoa slap into Spain. It would be tricky to find cover there, too, but he would see; he intended to be close by when Canisius went sailing over that bridge. If Anne-Marie saw him, and realized he had guessed her move, she would, at least, be disconcerted. She might not be put off, but the bare fact of seeing him would be grit in the wheels: it might, for instance, easily spoil her aim.

There came Canisius; talking to two other dim financial fellows, one doubtless the echo of himself, probably the Paris office of the

Sopexique. The other was more sunburnt, and much more wrapped up – local man, in a tweed jacket. Local manager or supervisor in charge of the building work, or possibly the architect. The city types were dressed the way city types do dress at seaside resorts full of palm trees and casinos and singing sunshine. Canisius made a marvellous target, thought Van der Valk gloomily; cream tussore suit like Mr Khruschev, oh dear, and a Panama hat! He was wearing straw-coloured plaited shoes too, and had something of Mr K's world-familiar waddle. The other, a smaller, thinner type with sleek shiny hair and a bald top, was fanning himself with his hat – in the sunshine it was a good twenty degrees, though it was still only March.

And the auto! That perhaps belonged to the Paris man; one of the gigantic six-litre Mercedes battleships that are longer than a Cadillac – and the top down! A chauffeur in riding boots and a peaked hat shaped like a German policeman's was holding doors open, and the porter of the Prince de Galles was making dignified fluttering movements and making sure there was no orange peel under the feet of his distinguished guests. The tweed coat got in at the front – the two from the Sopex at the very back. Van der Valk got a sudden sinking feeling as he thought that from nearly any of the hotel balconies it was a dead easy shot, a sitting cock pheasant if ever there was one. But no shot came: Anne-Marie had not booked in to the Prince de Galles.

The Mercedes rippled off with a noise like a woman's fingers smoothing a satin evening skirt and Van der Valk climbed into the hired Renault, which made a noise like a dock hand stacking empty oil drums, but the employees of the Prince de Galles were far too distinguished to look.

Keeping up was easy: the huge black car was very sedate. They slid through St Jean de Luz without as much as a toot, Van der Valk the regulation hundred metres in the rear, in his shirt sleeves. They crossed the bridge – but instead of sailing on along the coast to Hendaye the Mercedes suddenly swung abruptly to the left at a main road junction and Van der Valk grabbed at the Michelin on the seat beside him. Oh oh. There was another road, damn it, as well the National Ten, that skirted Hendaye and crossed the Bidassoa a kilometre lower down, the type of road described by guidebooks as 'picturesque stretch'. Which it was: here the foot-hills of the Pyrenees came down towards the narrow coastal strip where one squeezes through the Irun. A thick Mediterranean vegetation with cork oaks and umbrella pines was looking very springlike in the hot sunshine, though at the thousand metre level the snow was still waist deep. As the Mercedes slowed for the frontier post Van der Valk was realizing uneasily that the shooting cover was perfect. Nothing had happened, and nothing happened now. Yet the idea had taken possession of him in a way he recognized, for instead of a vaguely troubling theory he had a sudden wave of fierce feverish certainty: somewhere, somehow, there had been eyes along that road, eyes along a gun barrel.

He stopped the auto before the frontier. There had been no sign of the grey Opel, which could perfectly easily have passed into Spain. Here the hills took a dip into the valley of the Bidassoa, and the river, swollen now by the melting snow, passed under the bridge that formed the frontier. There was a tiny centre of activity around the customs house, where three or four autos were parked, a tricolour fluttered lazily in the puffs of pine-scented air off the hill, and the striped trousers of two customs men leaned together over the guardrail at the shoulder of the bridge, probably speculating about trout. Van der Valk backed the Renault on to a flattish strip of uneven ground, turned it, and felt sweat creeping down his spine, though it was not hot here. The sun was warm, yes, but a little breeze offshore was making the pine-trees whisper, and it came from the higher ground, where the snow still lay. There was goose-flesh on his bare arms: he wondered whether it came from the chilly little breaths of air, or that terrifying feeling of complete certainty. He was very tired, and was not certain whether his judgement was good. His shirt was soaking under his arms, which was a disagreeable feeling; he took his binoculars and tried to think coldly.

All along the road there were flat patches, a mixture of gravel, old pine-needles and a thin sprinkling of earth with coarse grass:

147

people in summer parked their autos there and climbed up to one of the ledges for a picnic. At the curves the road had been cut into the hillsides, and the shoulders were revetted with stone. The little watercourses running in irregular stony streaks down the slope vanished under the road in culverts that would all be dry in summer but were now active and talking.

As he looked he was not impressed by the possibility of a shot at an auto stopping for the frontier. It was a long shot, and blocked from too many angles. To get a clear sightline one would have to go too far back and too high, he thought. He was trying to see how he would have done it himself. Suppose that I were looking for a good place . . .

There was time in front of him. Canisius would not be back for several hours and one would have leisure to find a good spot. But he knew obscurely that the good spot had been found. It was not only the feeling of eyes somewhere that had made him sweat: he knew too that these plans cannot be carried out spontaneously. They need rehearsal. If he had been behind the gun he knew he would have let the big Mercedes pass unhindered too; the important thing was to get a good notion of how fast it went, what sort of target was presented, whether any unforeseen factor blocked the view and the shot. The woman was a skier; she knew something about terrain, about slopes and dips and humps of ground. She had the right blend of cold judgement to add to her boiling fury.

He started the motor and swung the boxy little Renault back the way he had come. There was little traffic on the road; it was too early in the year. The road led nowhere but into Spain, and plenty of people, especially the local people who had business over the border, took the coast road by the railway line. Duller but more direct. It was only later in the year that the floods of little cars like his and the big broad-bottomed touring coaches would be tempted by the 'pretty road'. People then would clamber in quantities up the dried watercourses and pick the aromatic leaves that smelt of turpentine and eucalyptus, and throw greasy bits of paper and beer cans around, and set the woods on fire too, no

148

doubt. There were notices in curly French lettering every couple of hundred metres. 'Fire is the woods' worst enemy. Your cigarette or your match can cause death and devastation. Negligence is criminal.'

At this time of year, the road was not even perfectly secure; the melting snow coursing down the steep slope that ran up in places almost vertically above the road could cause accidents that would not occur in summer. The falling water brought away loose stones and pebbles, bits of dead branch – occasionally even a tree might come down. Nothing really unsafe, of course; that would be seen to by Eaux et Forêts or Ponts et Chaussées or whoever the French authority was.

There ... Coming up a slope, and swinging out for a sharp bend, quite a large stone suddenly crashed on the roadway in front of him at a spot where the hill went up abruptly in a tangle of thin undergrowth. He braked and stopped. A stone the size of his two fists. There were a few pebbles and dead twigs on the road surface – but if that stone had landed on his bonnet ... He got out and went to look at the slope. It ran up for some fifteen metres over his head with little flat heathery bushes – some kind of broom? It was perfectly sound and safe, not crumbling or insecure looking in any way. It was hard to see where the stone had come from. He picked it up and tossed it over on to the valley side. He was walking back to the auto when the sweat started all over his body and he put his hand up in an unconscious gesture to his neck. He had stopped his car! Anybody within a hundred metres of him anywhere could have had a shot at him. He got into the driving seat and pressed his body hard back against the cushion, feeling his leg muscles strain and his shirt sticking to him. With an awkward hand – his fingers seemed difficult to articulate – he lit a cigarette. Then he got out of the auto again with a jump. The shot would not have come from anywhere within a hundred metres. It would come from where the stone had fallen.

The stone had not fallen: it had been thrown.

He stood still a long moment, the cigarette forgotten in his hand. The metal of the bonnet was warm and dusty under the other hand.

Anne-Marie Marschal could have been watching where the road forked in St Jean, she could have followed at her leisure. She would have seen the little Renault behind the whale-like Mercedes, but she had not looked at it: there were ten thousand such in France. There was nothing to connect him with it; when he had accompanied her it had always been in her own auto. When it had come back along the road it had meant nothing either. The stone – it had been a rehearsal . . .

But he had got out, and she had certainly seen him. The plan had been a good one; to throw a stone in front of the Mercedes – not big enough to cause a revolution, but enough to cause comment. Curiosity. Anybody would stop, slightly indignant, a little frightened – the chauffeur too would walk up and look in a puzzled way to see where it could possibly have come from, before tossing it over off the road, so as not to incommode other people. It had been well thought out, there would be a delay of two minutes, enough to lie down, take a careful unhurried sight – and send a bullet straight into Mr Khruschev's cream tussore bosom.

A sudden cold anger flamed in him. She had seen him – and he was the last person she wanted to see, the last person she would have chucked a stone at. Very well: the yob, the clot, the Dutch peasant, the illiterate nosy parker from the police was going to climb that slope.

He got into the auto, backed it with a grind and a tearing noise of little stones clear of the stream running along towards the next culvert, and let it go till he reached a patch where he could get it off the road altogether. He took his binoculars and started to walk forward, looking for a good place to climb, and stopped suddenly, thinking he heard a sound. It was hard to tell; the chuckle of water and the whisper of the wind in the boughs covered anything but a loud noise. A person moving would not necessarily be heard. He was not much of a scout; he hadn't even a gun. Old Shatterhand Van der Valk. He puffed and crashed through the undergrowth on the steep in a very un-Apache way.

But it was not difficult to find the place; all he had to do was to keep turning till he saw the road from exactly the right height and

150

distance. Near enough to toss a stone weighing a kilo or more, far enough back to have a comfortable shot – the range was not more than about forty metres. There were three more biggish stones collected, so that his was not, probably, the last rehearsal. She had practised too with pine cones, to get the exact moment at which to throw, to get the auto to stop at the right spot. Ten metres either way on the road did not make the shot more difficult; he could have been shot five times, and tossed over into the bushes on the other side. Quite likely he would have been. But she must have been disconcerted at seeing him. Would anyone even have heard the shots? She could have taken his auto. Where would hers be? Anywhere along the road – likely a kilometre away.

Nothing showed her presence; the pine needles had been scuffled, a twig broken. There was a handy branch to rest the gun barrel on. Sitting would be the best shot; one cannot lie well pointing downhill. A naughty little boy might have made the signs he found, a naughty little boy with a catapult. But he knew it was her; his sense there at the frontier, where he had spent an hour with his skin crawling had been so strong.

She must have gone uphill – there was no way back on to the road, or he would have noticed. She had had plenty of start. Behind the trees of the ridge that stuck out, forcing the road to make a loop, there was a higher, barer hill. If he went up that way he might see something. As long as he could keep her moving . . . He looked at his watch – it was after eleven already. Canisius would be back about three.

'Anne-Marie,' he shouted. 'Anne-Marie. It's useless. You won't get anything done this way.' His voice sounded thin and impotent, and higher up it might not even be heard: the wind was blowing against him, down the slope. Stalking from leeward – pretty inefficient, he told himself. But the underbrush was thinner already. He stopped, panting; he must be three hundred metres above sea level already, and working inland all the time.

As he thought, behind the ridge the ground went upwards at a much gentler angle but much longer. There were trees still but scattered. There were patches of tough grass that sheep or goats could graze on, and patches of rock showing at the steeper parts. Up at the top would be the snow line, probably – the timber was thicker again up there. He went on climbing, stopping to use his binoculars wherever he got a patch of open ground to look across. It was warmer up here, where the sun was not filtered through trees, and at the same time colder. The breeze was blowing straight off the snow line.

He never saw her at all; it was a wink of sudden intense light that caught his eye. It might have been metal, but it was more likely the lens on the telescopic sight that caught the sun for an instant and caused a reflection like a mirror. He looked through the binoculars but saw nothing: it must be her, though, he told himself. He had no idea of what he was doing and no particular fear: it was not as it had been on the road. He had forgotten the rifle altogether, very nearly, and when the shot came it took him by surprise in a way he would never have thought possible. There was physical surprise, if you can call it a surprise when something like a huge iron hand takes you full swing from nowhere in the middle of your body, and sends you crashing ten metres down the slope in a huddle of limp clothes with no breath or feeling left in you. Yet before he lost consciousness he had time to register the mental surprise of being shot. She's shot me, he told himself in a querulous, old-maidish voice. The stupid, stupid bitch. He felt pain from a graze on his nose and forehead – he had scraped himself falling.

Little idiot, he said. What will she do now, when she realizes she's killed me? Probably she'll know at least that she isn't a killer. She won't go back to her hide-out to wait for Canisius, now; probably she'll give herself up to the police. I don't particularly mind being killed, since it had to come some time. But it is very stupid. Nobody knows but me.

He went under.

*

'How do you feel?' asked Mr Lira. He had been taking Van der Valk over one point after another, never in a hurry, never surprised, never critical, writing slowly in a school exercise book in longhand.

Handwriting that was square, shapely, legible; like a school-master's.

'I feel all right. It's not disagreeable – like being a baby all over again. They roll you about and wash you and slap you and sit you on the pot and pin nappies on you. They enjoy it and I don't mind it – I just wonder how long it all goes on, that's all.'

'I had a colleague of yours in to see me. They're very filled with concern. They were agitated at your having come running down here, so I had to tell them a few things, which fluttered their pigeons a bit. They'll get a nice long report from me too. They won't be able to say you exceeded your instructions – they simply won't dare. I've also explained the facts of life to your financial friend.'

'Canisius?'

'Canisius. You never really got it clear, did you? How he'd worked it out. Why he insisted on you or someone like you.'

'No.'

'I read it all over and thought I saw it. So I made myself a bit scary – rattled chains at him a good deal. I got it out of him. He'd been told to hold himself at the disposition of the examining magistrate, and I sent him over a summons. Showed him the bullet – the one we got out the hillside below you. The one that went through Mrs Marschal,' said Lira drily, 'we left where it was. I put it on the desk, very melo, and asked him if he realized how easily it could have made a hole in him. Have you ever noticed? – you can't scare those ones with lawbooks – he knew all the law backwards, he'd done nothing the least illegal – but if you can frighten them physically they melt. He went like ice-cream in a hot sun.'

Van der Valk was entranced.

'I mustn't laugh because it hurts, but tell me.'

'Ah. Well, hearing all your tale, reading the report Strasbourg made, getting some dope on this Sopexique from Paris – there were a few points that struck me. The same things that worried you, the same things that bothered Strasbourg. Why was Canisius so insistent on getting a professional policeman? Why was he in such

a hurry, when the chap would certainly turn up sooner or later?
And so on.

'You've got to see it as a question of character. Canisius understood that couple pretty well. He caused as much friction as
possible. From one side, he bored and irritated Marschal as much
as he could with all the little petty trickeries and mean expedients
the business involved. If a competitor had to be attacked, he
brought Marschal into it. If a supplier had to be bribed, he got
Marschal to do it. And on the other side, he tickled the woman
every way he could think – knowing that she would be nagging at
Marschal continually to stand up for himself, to fight, to work at
the business and get some control of it instead of standing passive
and watching Canisius get the whole thing between his hands. He
even let the wife know that the old man in Paris was losing his
grip and that it was only a question of time before he and his pals
had absolute control. Sooner or later Marschal would just turn
his back and walk away – the wife knew that too. Neither of them
would have been very surprised when it happened.

'The idea of stirring up the police was simply a move to keep up
the pressure on Marschal. The woman, I think, couldn't make it
out, not at first, anyhow.'

'She was undecided,' said Van der Valk, thinking about Anne-
Marie in the house in Amsterdam. 'She would have liked to have
put a stop to it but she couldn't very well. Too official.'

'That was just the point. One reason why Canisius went to your
boss. He wanted a pompous, official rigid reaction. Another
reason may have been – I'm only guessing at this one – that a
professional of the criminal brigade would – just by nature of his
training – imagine that there was more to this than he had been
told, uh? Would go after Marschal wondering whether he was
going to find something fishy. There wasn't anything the least
fishy, but you would find it hard to believe that. I might be over-
estimating our friend here, but it has the sort of complex craftiness
I see in his character. When your bird really ran off with this girl
from Germany, it must have been a success past his wildest dreams.
Not only was Marschal behaving in a wild way, without foresight

154

or judgement, but he even did something technically criminal and stirred up all the police in Germany.

'Now I reckon then that Canisius was so confident he had it all in the bag that he couldn't resist ringing the wife up and taunting her with it.'

'No doubt about that. She went haywire. Jealousy as well – she was badly upset by the German girl. When I saw her there first in Austria she was more wild at that than anything else. Then she realized that I was more of a menace than she'd thought. Originally she'd counted on me to find Marschal, make him see a bit of sense, and get him to come home. She started to see me as an ally of Canisius, as a threat. She'd hoped I would lead her to Marschal, where she could talk to him, work on him, patch it all up. She tried to get me to go to bed with her – did I tell you that? When she realized that all she'd done was to make me more curious and more determined to find out what the hell was going on, she lost her head when it came to the point, and yelled at him. I thought for a while she might have got some message to him, through the bank perhaps. I doubt that now. I think when Marschal saw her there at the top of the ski-slope it was unexpected, and I think he was a lot more upset at seeing her than at seeing me. What could I do to him, really? – there wouldn't have been any real grounds for my making a fuss. I'd have seen to it the girl went home, sure. But I simply wanted to talk to him – find out what he thought about it all.'

'Her tragedy was that he thought of her as an enemy as great as Canisius. That was why she shot herself, in the long run. Why she shot you. Everything she touched turned to ashes. Finding that he'd killed himself in bed with that girl was a shock that put her completely off the rails. You know what I thought? Sounds lunatic to you perhaps, coming from someone like me. I think she didn't forgive his not killing himself in bed with her.'

'No,' said Van der Valk slowly. 'I don't find that lunatic. Not that there's any explanation needed. They were both doomed. The world we live in, it's the types like Canisius who win.'

'Canisius,' said Mr Lira, with a little smile as he thought about

155

that gentleman. 'I really scared him badly. And I got the reaction you'd expect from a type like that. You took his bullet. He's overflowing with conscience money: he'll make you a present of a couple of marshals any time. Not that the flow of generosity will last long,' drily.

'I couldn't care less about him. Let him arrange all the funerals – pleasant job for him.'

'You're wrong, my boy. I know how you feel, but you're wrong. I've talked to your wife. And I've taken the liberty of doing a bit of bargaining on your behalf. Your social security pays your hospital bill – but it doesn't pay you the pain. Maybe – I don't say it's sure or even probable – you have a bit of a disability. You get a pension payment – no no, don't quarrel with me, I'm a policeman myself, I know how these things go. Say they shove you out on pension, what would you get? How old are you, forty? Have you even twenty years' service? What would you get? Your wife told me. So don't get mad at me – I screwed your Mr Canisius a bit. The Marschal estate – I have this in writing – will triple any payment made you or your wife.'

'Give me a cigarette . . . What are they saying about me? Total disability?'

'They can't honestly say. They tell me that they're eighty per cent certain they'll put you on your feet as good as new – or nearly. I know Gachassin pretty well. If he said that he meant it. It's good – it isn't quite good enough.'

Van der Valk started to grin. 'All the same – how the hell did you manage to get a thing like that out of Canisius? He's tough – he can't have been that frightened.'

Mr Lira started to grin too.

'No – he wasn't. Not of me. It was your wife did it. Nice woman, your wife. I'd asked her to the office when he was there – I wanted to see the two of them together.' His grin broadened. 'She did fine.'

'What did she say?' Van der Valk knew that Arlette, in the push, was capable of anything. Not unlike Anne-Marie Marschal.

'She walked straight up to him,' said Lira with great enjoyment, 'and said for two pins she'd shoot him herself. And he saw she meant it, what's more. I tell you there's nothing like a bit of physical fear to cut those ones down to size. Every woman he sees for the rest of his life he's going to look at and wonder.'

Van der Valk started to laugh. It hurt so much he had to stop, but it was worth it.

'How does it strike you – finally? I made a mess of it. I make a hell of a fool of myself – look where it puts me – in a plaster coffin.'

Mr Lira tucked his exercise book under his arm and shook his head.

'Nothing strikes me. What does one ever do, knowing it to be the right thing?' He shook hands. The door opened and he looked up, but it was Arlette. 'Hallo, Madame, how are you? No no, I'm just going. All finished. When you're up' – to Van der Valk – 'we'll go fishing.' He stopped at the door and snapped his fingers. 'There's a phrase I'm trying to remember. La Bruyère. The one they give out to tease the philosophy students with. I got it as theme for my baccalauréat – my God, forty years ago.'

Van der Valk looked blank.

'I know it,' said Arlette with a laugh. She had come over to the bed to give him a kiss. 'You don't know it, my poor wolf, you're too Dutch. *Tout est dit . . .* '

'Everything is said and we come too late . . . '

'Since more than seven thousand years, since men exist, and think.'

Van der Valk began to laugh again.

'We'll drink to that – the three of us. The moment I'm on one foot.'

'Shouldn't we invite Canisius?' asked Arlette, maliciously.

More about Penguins and Pelicans

Penguinews, which appears every month, contains details of all the new books issued by Penguins as they are published. From time to time it is supplemented by *Penguins in Print*, which is a complete list of all titles available. (There are some five thousand of these.)

A specimen copy of *Penguinews* will be sent to you free on request. For a year's issues (including the complete lists) please send 50p if you live in the British Isles, or 75p if you live elsewhere. Just write to Dept EP, Penguin Books Ltd, Harmondsworth, Middlesex, enclosing a cheque or postal order, and your name will be added to the mailing list.

In the U.S.A.: For a complete list of books available from Penguin in the United States write to Dept CS, Penguin Books Inc., 7110 Ambassador Road, Baltimore, Maryland 21207.

In Canada: For a complete list of books available from Penguin in Canada write to Penguin Books Canada Ltd, 41 Steelcase Road West, Markham, Ontario.